# THE WHORE NEXT DOOR

## Welcome to Thotville

By

Sheena Perry

*Sheena Perry* PUBLISHING

## Copyright

The Whore Next Door

Copyright © 2020 Sheena Perry

Published by Sheena Perry Publishing

Edited by Sheena Perry

ISBN-10: 1-950618-04-8
ISBN-13: 978-1-950618-04-0

## The *Tea* on the Author

Sheena Perry is originally from Dallas, TX. She was raised by her teenage single mother, Tonya. Sheena is the oldest of two children. Sheena's mother fell prey to the booming crack cocaine era of the 1980's. Entrusting a close relative with the task of babysitting her two kids, Tonya left for work one day not realizing that the family member would leave them alone and call DCFS.

At tender age of three, Sheena and her brother were removed from the home and placed into separate foster homes. While her brother was placed into a fairly nice foster home, she however suffered unimaginable abuse at the hands of her foster parents. She went days without eating, was fed dog food and she was tied to a chair throughout the day. Her thighs are still branded with the markings from the tight ropes.

Her mother was able to quickly regain custody of both children. However, later the same year she was molested by her mother's fiancé. Immediately reporting the abuse to her mother, the monster was quickly apprehended and served a lengthy stint in prison. Prison did not stop Sheena's molester from issuing out death threats.

He was heavily involved in the drug world and his threats were taken very seriously. Sheena's mom relocated her small family to Columbus, GA. After experiencing such traumatic events, she became extremely shy and withdrawn. She was even mute for two years. The once bubbly outgoing little girl had been replaced by an insecure, self-loathing shell of her former self.

As she became older, Sheena would contemplate suicide numerous times to cope with the unfortunate cards she had been dealt. She had even developed an eating disorder in her mid-teens. Sheena's mother continued to battle with her drug addiction throughout her childhood and into her young adulthood. Sheena has always had a deep passion for reading and writing. Reading has always been her outlet to escape the obstacles that she faced on a daily basis.

She enjoys romance, mystery, horror, autobiographies, thrillers and urban novels. From an early age, Sheena had tutored kids much older than herself. Sheena particularly enjoys writing short stories and poetry. She currently lives in Florissant, MO. Despite her rough beginnings, she was able to conquer all of her hurdles and meet many of her goals.

She was able to purchase her first house at the age of 20. A year later she gave birth to her daughter, Aaliyah. Somehow, she managed to overcome the murder of her daughter's father, who was killed by the police when their daughter was just 4 months old. She is a Registered Nurse. Sheena has a master's degree in Nursing Education. She is currently in school pursing her Doctorate degree.

She works as a nursing professor at a major university and is the Director of Nursing at a long-term care facility. Sheena is also a licensed foster parent. Having had such a horrific experience during her time in foster care, she wanted to offer a safe home to children in need.

Please stay tuned for *Inevitable Deceptions: The Heart's Journey to Nowhere 3* which is Sheena's third and final installment of the series. She also co-wrote the children's book *I Made You From Scratch: You Are Perfect* with her daughter.

In addition to Inevitable Deceptions: *The Heart's Journey to Nowhere 3*, she is currently working on two other books: *Do No Harm: License to Kill and Help! I Ate Peanuts, Now My*

***Throat's Swelling Up!*** She has also published novels such as ***The Girl Behind The Smile*** by Dornisha Goodrich, ***God Showed Me More Than Heaven*** by K.S. Fisher and ***The Living*** by Frank Washington. Please stay tuned!

*I attribute my success to this – I never gave or took any excuse. – Florence Nightingale*

## Connect with Sheena

Visit her website at www.sheenaperrypublishing.com

Friend her on Facebook at www.facebook.com/sheena.p.rn

Link with her on LinkedIn at
www.linkedin.com/in/sheena-perry-msn-rn-cne-22352486

Follow her on Twitter at www.twitter.com/sheenamperry

Follow her on Instagram at www.instagram.com/sheenamperry

You can also visit her business page at
https://m.facebook.com/SheenaPerryPublishing/

Check out her work on
https://www.amazon.com/Sheena-Perry/e/B06XBSPTXP/ref=ntt_dp_epwbk_0

Submissions for all genres are now open. Please submit the first 3-4 chapters of your manuscript for publishing consideration. Allow up to 30 days for a response. Complete contact information including name, address, contact number and email. Use 12 pt. font, double-spaced in manuscript style format. Email manuscripts to submissions@sheenaperrypublishing.com.

We look forward to hearing from you!

## Dedication

I'd like to dedicate this book to all of those who have been on the receiving end of abuse. Always know that it is never your fault. You are not alone. Don't be ashamed. Be your own advocate; seek help immediately before it is too late. Do not let your abuser have power over you. Remember that if they've abused you once, chances are that they will strike again.

In loving memory of Michael Calvin Perry, Doris Marie Green, Carolyn Marie White, James Green, Samuel Keita DeBoise, Erin LeighAnna Nabe, Lennette Berry, Michael Perry, Jr, Paul Anthony Sheets, Sr and Pauline Roberts-Perry.

I love and miss you all more than anyone will ever know. Rest in paradise.

~Sheena

## Table of Contents

## Acknowledgements

To my loving mother, Tonya Perry, I appreciate you for always being my biggest cheerleader. You have always inspired me to challenge myself. You are the strongest person that I know. I love you so much Ma!

To my brother, Rico, we may not always see eye to eye but know that I will always love you to the moon and back. No one can make me laugh the way that you do. You are my best friend.

To my beautiful daughter, Aaliyah, the day that I had you was by far the happiest day of my life. You made me grow up overnight. You are growing into the most amazing young woman that I could ever ask for. I know that your dad is smiling down at you from heaven. I hope that I have always been a positive role model for you and that you realize that you are my biggest motivator. All of my accomplishments were achieved with you in mind. Remember the sky is the limit and that the word *never* is not a part of our vocabulary. I love you baby girl.

To my friends and colleagues that have put up with my endless brainstorms and offered words of encouragement, I thank you for everything. I'd also like to thank my test readers who have given me constructive criticism.

I'd also like to give a special thanks to my readers who have purchased, downloaded and rated my books. You will never know how much your love and support mean to me.

Lastly, I'd like to thank the good Lord above. Thank you for continuing to bless me. Without you, none of this would be possible.

~Sheena

# *****WARNING*****

# THIS NOVEL CONTAINS STRONG LANGUAGE, BROKEN ENGLISH, SEX, VIOLENCE, AND VULGAR SITUATIONS WHICH MAY BE OFFENSIVE TO SOME READERS.

# « Chapter 1 Thick Is In, Fat Is Out »

"**RUN RAE! RUN!!!**" Desirae Sanchez's classmates screamed out to her.

Desirae was extremely winded as she hobbled around the seemingly never-ending school track. Her lungs were scorching as she struggled to breathe in the summer air. Very few places rival that intense Texas heat. Beads of sweat dripped down her forehead quicker than she could swipe them away.

A few of them had managed to make it into her eyes burning them with their salty composition. She wanted to cry with every dry rub that her inner thighs made whenever they connected. Since she had forgotten to apply some baby powder in between her meaty thighs, they now felt as if she were being rug burned with every painful step she took.

Desirae absolutely hated gym class and most of all she hated running. Or whatever it was that she was currently doing.

As much as she wanted to just give up and stop the very activity that was causing her so much agony, she didn't want to let her teammates down.

At fifteen, Desirae stood at five foot four inches, however, she tipped the scales at a whopping two hundred and fifty-five pounds. She was a big girl for sure and felt every single ounce of it. Luckily, she was paired up against another overweight classmate who fortunately for Desirae appeared to be struggling just a little bit more than she was.

After what seemed like hours, Desirae finally tapped her classmate's hand who then took off around the track with lightning speed. Desirae was ecstatic that her team was in the lead and was pretty much guaranteed to win the race, however she was even happier that she could finally stop running. As she painfully limped over to the bleachers, she prayed to God that she made it there without passing out.

When she finally made it over to the bleachers, she happily plopped down and reached for her water bottle. Removing the cap, she guzzled the cool liquid until the bottle was empty. She had never tasted anything better than that water in that very moment. She felt that she might actually live after all once she had quenched her thirst. As she watched the race conclude, she couldn't help but to long for the moment when she graduated and could leave her dreadful high school behind.

Desirae had a gorgeous face. She was Dominican and African American, which gave her the most beautiful chocolate complexion. Her thick eyebrows overlooked her almond shaped hazel eyes. Her high cheekbones gave Lela Rochon a run for her money.

Her lips weren't all that big, yet they were perfectly sculpted. Her white teeth were currently covered by braces, but her teeth were almost perfect now and she would soon be ready for them to be removed. Her thin nose was adorned by a small diamond stud to her left nostril. She was lovely, yet her weight had always overshadowed her beauty.

The only thing that she was ever complimented on was her beautiful long tresses that nearly reached her ample bottom, but that was about it. Aside from hating gym, she was a great student academically.

She especially excelled in and loved science. For as long as she could remember, she knew that she wanted to become a dentist just like her parents. She was going to work for the family business one day. Although she was quiet and shy, she did have two best friends, Alonzo who everyone called Zo and Afrika.

The trio had been close since they were in elementary school. Rae was the quiet, shy one out of their crew while Zo and Afrika boldly spoke their minds. Zo was very cute. He was light complexioned with neatly cut curls spiraled all over his head. Light freckles peppered his handsome face. He had deep set dimples and a cleft chin. His dark brown eyes appeared to see through you. He was 6 feet tall and on the thin side.

He had come out of the closet back when they were in the seventh grade and hasn't looked back since. Luckily, he had a strong support system and both of his parents were accepting of his sexual orientation.

Afrika was a petite dark skin girl whose skin was so smooth that she sometimes appeared porcelain-like. She resembled African royalty. As you may have guessed, she and her mother were in fact from Africa...Kenya to be exact. Her mother immigrated to the Lone Star state to offer her daughter a better life. Afrika kept her hair braided, which she typically did herself.

Homegirl was gifted when it came to doing hair!

All she talked about was opening up her own beauty salon after they graduated. Rae and Zo were already best friends when Afrika transferred into their second-grade class. She initially was so timid and quiet when she came to school. She didn't wear the best clothes and their classmates made her painfully aware of it.

They teased her horribly about her dark skin, natural hair, thick accent, and her less than popular clothing. Rae and Zo had noticed her crying more times than they cared to remember. To them she had always been extremely beautiful. There was just something about her that they liked, and that part hated how the other kids messed with her.

Once Afrika joined their circle, they had subconsciously connected to one another by their perceived flaws. To others they were merely a fat girl, sissy boy and tacky African girl, but together they created a brother and sisterhood that no one could waver. They pulled their strength from one another and there was nothing that anyone could say to change it.

In her homeroom, Rae couldn't seem to keep her eyes off of Prosper Collins. That boy just melted her heart every time she laid eyes on him. He was the color of butterscotch with the most seductively intense eyes she'd ever laid eyes on. While he probably wasn't the finest thing walking the halls of Malcolm X Academy to everyone, he certainly was in her eyes.

Perhaps his most attractive attribute was his crazy sense of humor. To say that he was the class clown would be an understatement. One thing that she respected about him was the fact that even when other students were dishing fat jokes her way, he never participated and instructed them to stop.

She'd never held a conversation with Prosper before, but she spent quite a bit of her classroom time caressing him with her gaze. She wished that she were more like the other girls so that he would show her some attention. What girl didn't like a funny guy? With that being said, he was always surrounded by girls. Unfortunately for Rae, none of them looked like her in the slightest bit.

## « Chapter 2 The Masterplan »

MANY SAY THAT SOME of the seemingly happiest people are often times also the saddest. Behind many smiles lie a great deal of gloom. This could be said for Prosper Collins. It made his day to ensure that those around him were happy, even at the expense of his own happiness. He was a people pleaser, always had been. Prosper had a heart of gold and luckily for everyone around him, he didn't allow his personal circumstances to change that. His charm and good sense of humor afforded him the attention that he never received at home.

At school he could be a carefree teenager, but at home he acted as the sole caregiver for his little sister, Serena. He had actually been the one to name his three-year-old sister. Since he had been crushing on Serena Williams his entire life, he couldn't think of a nobler name. Prosper was only twelve when his drunken mother gave birth to Serena and he hadn't stopped looking out for her since. Often times Prosper had to correct the confused child when she referred to him as dad.

Unlike most teenagers his age, Prosper wasn't afforded the luxury of hanging out after school. After school he had to rush to pick up his sister from his cousin. Although his mom didn't work and was usually at home, she didn't want to be bothered by the inquisitive child.

To be honest, Prosper didn't trust his mother with her for extended periods of time anyway. He knew that she wouldn't intentionally harm his sister, but it was the unintentional negligence that worried him. After school his days were spent cooking, cleaning the house, doing homework, bathing his sister and tucking her in at night. The routine would then repeat itself the following day.

What many people didn't know about the funny teenager was that he was incredibly bright. He had never earned less than an A on his report cards throughout the years. He was one of those people who rarely had to study in order to perform well. He was definitely the man at school.

His mom, Shawn, received government assistance, alimony and child support from both of her kid's fathers, so financially they were able to get by. Alcohol was relatively cheap in relation to drugs, so Shawn allowed Prosper to take over the money and household bills. As long as there was always money to keep her wasted, she didn't care about the rest.

Shawn wasn't always an alcoholic. It was actually her ex-husband Arriyon who was also Serena's dad who had driven her to drink. Arriyon was an extremely successful real estate agent who unfortunately couldn't keep his dick in his pants. Shawn had devoted six years of her life into attempting to change a man into something he simply wasn't destined to be. While she loved him deeply, she also loved the stability he was able to provide.

It didn't take long before Shawn began to rely on Mr. Whiskey to keep her company. It was her alcohol that kept her company during the long nights she was up waiting for Arriyon to find his way home. One of the many things that Shawn regretted during her rare sober moments was dragging her twin sister, Dawn, down with her. Of course, her biggest regret of all was not being well enough to care for her children.

Eventually she found the strength to finally leave Arriyon. With all of the evidence of his numerous affairs and love child, the female judge awarded Shawn their beautiful five-bedroom home as well as hefty alimony and child support payments. Outwardly life for the small family appeared to be peachy, but just like the phony smiles mentioned before…things weren't always what they seemed.

Prosper talked to a girl who worked in the mall and through her employee discount, he kept him and Serena looking nice. Sometimes Prosper felt as if he were living a double life.

Despite being popular at school, Prosper was a loner as soon as that final bell rang. It's not that things had to be that way; he just didn't want people to see how messed up his mom was most of the time. He feared that someone would report her to child protective services and Serena would be lost in the system. He'd die before he'd let that happen. To avoid the fuckery, he decided to keep his circle nonexistent.

The only exception to that rule was his first cousin, Charlie. The only reason Charlie was able to penetrate Prosper's bubble was because their mothers often got drunk together. Charlie, who was an only child, understood Prosper's struggles. Charlie was perhaps the only person in the world that he trusted, but Charlie was always getting into shit.

Every day Charlie was coming up with some stupid get rich scheme and Prosper often found himself in the midst of his bullshit too. Charlie was determined to strike it rich one day and Prosper knew that with his ambition the sky was the limit for him.

Charlie had quit school once he reached sixteen. He felt that it was a waste of time and prevented him from getting to the money. He knew early on that a nine to five would never satisfy him. He dreamed much bigger than that. It is Charlie who watched Serena while Prosper attended school during the day. He was good with her and Prosper knew that Charlie loved Serena as much as he did.

Although Charlie was older than Prosper by a year, Prosper acted like the older one. Charlie sold a little weed to get by, but he knew that shit wouldn't get him where he dreamed of being either.

One day Charlie burst into Prosper's room yelling that he had yet another plan for them to strike it big. Prosper rolled his eyes to the heavens, but as usual he listened to his cousin because he knew that he wouldn't leave until he did.

"So, I'm fucking with this bitch who is mad at her nigga for beating on her and guess what the bitch tells me? She told me that the nigga has a safe with a quarter of a mil in there! And guess what? Nigga, guess what?!" Charlie exclaimed when Prosper's thirst didn't match his own

"What muthafucka? What?!" Prosper asked finally feigning excitement. Fake or not, Charlie didn't care.

"The bitch knows the code!!!" Charlie squealed a few too many octaves for Prosper's liking.

"Nigga, you are sounding really Mariah Carey-ish right

now. Breathe a little and calm your happy ass down. How do you know that you can trust this broad? She could be setting your gullible, pussy whipped ass up. What's in it for her?" Prosper asked getting serious.

His cousin had a tendency to jump headfirst into shit without thoroughly planning things out correctly. He just thought of the gains…never the risks.

Charlie blinked a couple of times at Prosper before yelling, "Well, nigga if you would just shut your funny looking ass up for a minute, I'd tell you. I was getting there…damn!"

Knowing that his cousin could act like an overgrown spoiled brat, Prosper threw his hands up in the air and let his cousin finish hashing out his plan.

"So, get this, the bitch doesn't want any of the cash, she only wants the coke and jewelry in that safe. My nigga! That's one hundred and twenty-five thousand dollars each!!!"

"Soooo…what's your plan?" Prosper asked. Even he had to admit that the money sounded good.

He temporarily thought of all the things that he could do with that kind of money.

"Basically, we will set it up to where we wear ski masks and meet the bitch as she comes home and gets out of her car. We will have her at gun point. That will explain how we gained access to the house. I'll rough her up a little bit for the security cameras inside and then tie her up. We will ransack the place and conveniently stumble across the safe.

We will then "force" the safe's code out of her. We will get the money, coke and jewelry from the safe and bounce leaving her tied up. After shit cools off, I'll meet up with the bitch and give her the coke and jewelry." Charlie stated matter-of-factly.

Prosper pursed his lips and just glared at his cousin as if in deep thought.

The anticipation was killing Charlie. Just as he was about to speak Prosper asked, "Where will her nigga be?"

"That's the best part cuzzo! That nigga is going out of town on a business trip tomorrow night! The maid will find and untie shorty the morning after."

Giving his cousin a once over Prosper said, "Well it's about damn time you came up with a halfway decent plan! Let's do this shit tomorrow night!"

# « Chapter 3 White Lies »

"**HAPPY BIRTHDAY BIG** head!!!" Rae's brothers yelled startling her from her restful sleep.

"Oh God, what time is it? Rae groggily asked.

Anthony and Samuel were both in town from college for the weekend to celebrate their little sister's sweet sixteen. At twenty-three, Ant was the oldest of the close-knit trio. Sam was twenty-one. Both were in school gearing up for the family dentistry business. The Sanchez parents couldn't be prouder of their children.

Their mother, Valentina was Dominican, however, she was born and raised in Texas. Valentina's parents wanted her to disassociate herself from her roots and tried their damndest not to teach her Spanish, however, the intelligent child picked it up easily and was thankful as it helped tremendously in her line of work. Unlike her parents, she made sure that her children spoke both Spanish and English fluently. Now that they were older, they rarely spoke Spanish at home out of respect for her husband, James Sanchez...who although he was African American had a traditionally Hispanic surname.

James tried to learn a little Spanish over the years, but it just never quite stuck with him. While he understood much of it from hearing his wife and children speaking it over the years, he just felt foolish when he actually attempted to articulate it. It just wasn't for him. To keep it simple they just spoke English in his presence.

Valentina and James lived modestly. They could've afforded a much flashier lifestyle, however, they were practical people and didn't feel the need to flaunt their money to keep up with the Joneses. Their children wanted for nothing. They were all smart, healthy, and they all had great teeth. The only child that sometimes worried them was Desirae. Their only daughter and youngest child was the apple of their eye. She had always been a little princess, but not in a bratty way.

Her dad and big brothers had always been her protectors, but with them away at school she seemed more reserved and withdrawn. The sadder she seemed, the more weight she seemed to gain. She ate normal portions during mealtimes, so her parents were certain that she was a closet eater. They tried to enroll her into different weight loss programs, but she never stuck with any of them.

Eventually they decided to back off a little. After all, Valentina herself was a little on the plump side. She had managed to slim down while she was in high school and only regained her weight after she started having her babies. James never cared or made her feel insecure, so she just went on with their life.

It was now Rae's sixteenth birthday and they had special plans for her that day. It was a Saturday so after her brothers woke her up, she decided to take a shower and to get dressed for her day. The first smell of pancakes, bacon, eggs and oatmeal infiltrated her nose as she decided to follow the delicious aromas into the kitchen. There she was greeted by her amazing family.

They all greeted her with warm hugs and loving kisses to the forehead. Rae beamed with excitement for several reasons, one of them being the fact that her big brothers were home. The other reason of course was the fact that she was a little closer to finishing high school.

They all talked and ate, and it felt good to have the whole clan around the same table again. After breakfast, Valentina planned to take Rae out for a girl's day at the spa. They were going to get their hair done, manicures, pedicures, massages and waxes. Following the spa date, the two headed out to do a little retail therapy. By the time they finished, they each had arm loads of bags and were pooped.

Rae was no fool. Although she had told her family that she didn't want to have a party, she knew that they were going to throw one anyway. It was confirmed when both of her besties showed up dressed to kill and urged her to do the same. Deciding that protesting would be useless, she decided to shower again being careful not to get her newly acquired straight hair wet. When she got out of the shower, her besties had already taken the liberty of placing the outfit that she was to wear on the bed.

After she moisturized her skin, she put on the soft lavender dress that covered her bed. It was a beautiful dress she supposed, but somehow plus sized clothes and large shoes lost their appeal after a certain size. Rarely did it resemble its originally intended blueprint. Rae avoided looking in the mirror because she knew that she'd refuse to leave her room once her full-length mirror revealed her truth. Afrika came in and beat her face to absolute perfection. She couldn't stop staring at her face.

Afrika and Zo knew that she was pleased with the results when she suddenly began to snap selfies and posted them on social media. They hung out in her room as they had done thousands of times before in the past. Rae knew that they were trying to distract her and keep her in her room while her family set up her party. Again, being the team player that she was, she obeyed.

"Zo! Why are you over there looking so guilty? Spill the tea hunty!" Afrika exclaimed being extra as usual. Her once strong accent was now barely detectable.

"Bitch, what do you mean?! I'm over here living my best life." He chuckled guiltily.

"Unh Unh...I agree with Afrika. You reek of deceit!" Rae chimed in.

"Fine! Fine! Okay with yalls nosy asses! But you can't tell noooooooobody!" Zo exclaimed looking worried.

Rae and Afrika both looked at one another and fell out laughing.

"Bruh! Who the fuck are we gonna tell?! We are all here!" They both scolded their ditzy friend in unison.

Zo was without a doubt one of the smartest people that they knew, but he was no stranger to having infamous blonde moments.

Scratching his head, he simply stated, "Oh yeah. My bad. So, as I was saying, I've had my cherry popped! I ain't no virgin no more chile!"

Again, both girls made eye contact before attacking their bestie with a barrage of questions.

"When? Who? How? Well actually, I know how, but where? How was it? Did you like it? Did it hurt? Would you do it again? Was it better than a Popeyes chicken sandwich???" Both girls questioned mercilessly without breathing.

Zo just smirked as he momentarily relived his experience. He patiently answered each of his best friends' questions.

"It happened yesterday. Do you know Luis on the football team?"

Rae interrupted, "Fine ass Luis with the dimples?! I didn't know he was gay...or bi."

"Bitch please, you'd be surprise at how many of those thirsty ass niggas have tried to get some of this 'bussy' on the low." Zo confidently bragged while twerking until a sharp pain shot through his freshly deflowered asshole reminding him to sit his fast ass still.

"I guess the grimace on your face just answered whether or not that shit hurt." Afrika squealed.

"Hell, yes that shit hurt like hell, but in a good way...if that makes sense."

"No nigga, that shit makes no sense at all." Rae denied.

"You'll see what I mean one day when y'all decide to give up y'alls little cats. Anyway, do y'all want me to finish or not, damn?! This story has an expiration date bitches. As I was saying before I was so very rudely interrupted, Luis has been trying to part these cheeks and bend me over since the beginning of the school year. I've basically been teasing the absolute fuck out of him. That nigga be Doordashing me food and shit damn near every day trying to court a bitch.

He's been inviting me over and shit, but I've been scared. Finally, he texted me a picture of some fried chicken and Mac and cheese that he had made. He told me that his mom was working the overnight shift at the hospital and he wanted some company. Never being one to turn down fried chicken, I decided to kiss my cherry goodbye because I knew that I would not be returning with that bitch. I got all cute and he sent an Uber for me.

I walked into his house and it was all clean and smelled good. He was walking around in just some grey sweats on. He wasn't playing fair, friends!" Zo gulped really hard for the dramatics before continuing. The girls were eating it up!

"After we ate, he grabbed me by my hand and led me to his bedroom. He had a dope ass king sized bed. We kissed for a while and then we started jerking each other off. Just before he came, he started to undress me. I don't want to be too graphic, but it did hurt when he bent me over.

After it was over, we slept in each other's arms. I had to sneak out of course before his mom got home and caught us. Yes, I would most certainly do it again. And yes, it is better than a Popeyes chicken sandwich, yet not quite as good as a Chick-fil-a sandwich."

The girls stared at their friend in stunned silence. They had never heard of a more romantic first time in their entire lives. Hell, neither had Zo. He very well couldn't tell the girls that his first time had actually been with Luis bent over in his old ass Honda Accord.

While it was true that a lot of the guys wanted to sample him, all Luis had to do was discreetly grab Zo's ass and he followed his sexy ass outside. It was just a little white lie. The who and the act didn't waver and that was all that mattered.

## « Chapter 4 Silent Savior »

AFTER ZO GAVE THE GIRLS his slightly embellished tale of losing his virginity, it was time for Rae's not so surprise party to begin. Lavender was Rae's favorite color, so of course the theme of the party was lavender and white. Her family had done an amazing job with the decorations and her birthday cake of course fit into the theme as well.

Although Rae didn't have many friends, having her two besties at her side was everything to her. Rae did however have a huge family on both sides so there was a house full of guests there to celebrate her special day with her. Her big brother, Ant swore that he was a DJ, so he kept all the good music coming.

Afrika and Zo danced until their little hearts were content, while Rae in true form remained a wallflower. Although she was not the excitable type, Rae did however, thoroughly enjoy her birthday party. She opened up all of her presents and thanked everyone individually, but the best surprise had yet to come.

Just as Rae thought the party was over, she was blindfolded and guided outside to the front porch. It was Sam who assisted her carefully down the five steps that led up to their house. Suddenly, Rae was asked to remove her blindfold and when she did, she let out such a loud scream that people from five miles away probably heard her.

There parked in their driveway was a 2016 Nissan Maxima and of course it was lavender with silver glitter throughout the paint. It was absolutely gorgeous. It may have been gaudy and too girly for many people, but for Rae it was her absolute dream car.

Rae hadn't cried that hard in years. Her mom literally had to come over and wipe the snot that rested on her upper lip away from her face. Once she composed herself, she was then able to thank everyone again for giving her the best sweet sixteenth birthday any girl had ever experienced, at least in her mind.

After collecting her car keys and ripping the bow off of her brand-new car, Rae and her two besties took off to joyride in her new vehicle. Afrika was the only one out of the three who already had a vehicle.

Zo was too scary to learn how to drive so for now they would have to get Zo to and from his destinations. After the trio had their fair share of sightseeing and riding around the city, Rae decided that she was exhausted considering how she had been going since earlier that morning in preparation for her special day. She dropped her friends off at Afrika's vehicle and from there, Afrika took Zo home.

By the time she got home her house was quiet and dark. She assumed that her family was exhausted if not more exhausted than she was, since they had to do all the decorating and arrangements for her party. Her brothers' rental car was missing, so she knew that they were out partying like most college students tended to do. She also noticed that she still had some cake left over so she decided to cut a hefty piece. She then sat out on the front porch to enjoy the nice cool breeze outside. Honestly, she wanted to stare at her car in the driveway too.

Pulling out her iPhone she decided to post more pictures of her special day...especially of her brand-new car. Rae was on cloud nine and all of her issues and unhappiness dissipated in the moment. She decided to open up her Kindle Unlimited app and began to read *My Brother's Lady, My Baby* 1 by that new dope author Sheena Perry.

In the mist of reading that page turner, Rae heard a loud commotion coming from down the street followed by what sounded like firecrackers. She cautiously stood up on high alert and saw a figure collapse onto the pavement, while another figure momentarily looked over their shoulder. The standing figure soon snapped out of their trance and continued to run further into the darkness and towards her house.

Once the figure came into complete focus, Rae zeroed in on who it was and motioned for him to come over. She wasn't sure what was transpiring, yet she knew he needed her help. She didn't speak to him, however, she did place her right index finger up to her lips in order to prompt the visitor to remain silent. He appeared to be worried and traumatized as he kept looking back towards the other figure that remained lying motionless on the sidewalk.

At one point, he attempted to run back towards the direction from which he came, however, Rae even shocked herself when she intervened and pulled him through her front door. She cautiously glanced around her quiet house to make sure that all was still tranquil.

Rae remained silent as she led the visitor up to her bedroom, careful not to make any loud noises. There was no need to call for medical assistance as her nosy neighbors had already taken care of that task. Rae could hear an ambulance headed their way in the near distance.

Prosper didn't speak as he stood in the middle of the girl's room. She had so many questions, but decided that he'd share what was going on when he was ready. She noticed that he was carrying a large bag in his left hand and as soon as he noticed her looking down at it, he laid it down on her dresser. Rae could see tears streaming down his stressed face and the only thing she could think to do was to wrap her arms around him hoping to be a comfort in some way.

Luckily, her parents were both fairly deep sleepers so the commotion down the street didn't seem to rouse them. Still she cautiously locked her door and pulled back her lavender bedspread for the handsome visitor to lay down on. He instinctively removed his shoes followed by his black hoodie and jeans. Rae blushed at the sight of Prosper's sexy body clad in only boxers and a white t-shirt. Luckily deep in his own thoughts, he didn't seem to notice…or so Rae thought.

She knew that it was still too dangerous for him to leave in that moment and that his best chance at survival was probably for him to stay until the morning. Then she would be able to sneak him out and take him to wherever his destination was. They both laid awake through most of the night with him silently crying and her lovingly watching over him to make sure that he was okay. She only knew that he was crying because of the way his broad shoulders occasionally shook.

As the sun began to rise, he finally turned over to face her. She wasn't sure if he had ever looked at her before, but his piercing eyes barely blinked as he focused on her features. He studied her eyebrows, her lips and then her chin before finally stroking her jet-black hair. She was enjoying every second of his affection, unfortunately she knew that it would soon all be over.

As the sun begin to creep in, she sat up on the side of her bed and gave him a knowing look. He obediently followed her lead without question. He then snatched up his bag which had been lying on the dresser and together they cautiously tiptoed back out of the house. When Rae walked up to her new car, Prosper looked at her and then her vehicle with a nod of approval. She blushed and allowed him to get in.

He typed his destination into her car's GPS and she proceeded to follow its directions. Rae was immediately disheartened when they arrived at a house approximately fifteen minutes later. She put the car in park and they just sat there in complete silence. Luckily, he didn't make an effort to reach for the door handle. It was almost as if he was dreading getting out and going into his house.

After several minutes of awkward silence, Prosper finally turned to face Rae and leaned in slowly as if he were about to kiss her. Suddenly a couple of guys from school ran up to the car and started motioning for him to get out of her car. Prosper looked at her regretfully as he turned to get out, yet almost immediately he directed his full attention to the guys. He walked away without speaking so much as a single word to her.

## « Chapter 5 The Aftermath »

**RAE SLOWLY PULLED AWAY** from Prosper's house in tears. She didn't expect his departure to be so abrupt...so cold. What exactly did she expect? She wasn't altogether sure, but she knew the way that it all went down, wasn't it. Where was his gratitude for her potentially saving his life?

Her perfect birthday had ended even more perfectly because she was able to finally spend time with the guy of her dreams. It ended on such a good note and now he had to go and burst her bubble. She had promised herself a month ago that after her birthday she would finally make an effort to exercise more and to eat healthier. Now that notion was thrown out when she found herself in a Burger King drive-thru line ordering shit that meant her no good.

When she went to retrieve her purse from the floor of the passenger side of her vehicle, she noticed that Prosper had left the large bag that he had been toting around with him.

"Damn." Rae mumbled.

She damn sure wasn't about to bring it back to his ungrateful ass right now. She'd see him in their homeroom class and return it then.

"Screw him." She stated out loud as she picked up her purse to pay for her food.

Once she had her food in hand, she decided to pull into a parking space and eat her food there. She had told her mother about her post-birthday resolutions and didn't want to disappoint her with her unhealthy food choices. As she greedily scarfed down her food, she became numb to the pain. The tater tots worked like a pain pill releasing her endorphins. She ate even after she was no longer hungry because she couldn't stomach the idea of wasting food.

As the last sip of her sprite made its way down her esophagus, the pain almost instantaneously returned. Defeated, she put her car in gear and discarded the evidence of her guilt into one of the many pull-up trash cans in the parking lot. She then slowly made her way home.

Back at Prosper's house, two dudes that he was cool with who had also lived nearby had heard about Prosper missing. They were out scouting the neighborhood for Prosper per Shawn's request. When asked, they weren't sure of Charlie's status, so he thanked them for their concern, dapped them up and made a beeline for his front door.

He wasn't trying to be rude, but for the first time that day, he realized that he had left Serena alone with Shawn overnight. His heart pounded in his throat as he unlocked and then opened the front door. Rushing into the living room, he stopped dead in his tracks when he saw a seemingly sober Shawn braiding Serena's hair. In the recliner sat Charlie's goofy ass smiling like the cat who swallowed the canary. The stress of the previous night all came flooding back and Prosper broke down. He wasn't even ashamed of the tears that flowed freely down his face. Shawn and Serena both rushed to his side while Charlie looked on knowingly.

Charlie had also shed his fair share of tears not only over his near-death experience, but also for his cousin who had seemingly disappeared. He thought that he had gotten caught up.

Thinking back over the previous night, things were unfolding beautifully. Shorty arrived in front of her house on time, he had held her at gun point with the fake gun he'd spray painted just for the occasion. He roughed her up as promised, while Prosper ransacked the house. Life was beautiful. Prosper gave an Oscar award winning performance when he had "inadvertently" discovered the large safe tucked away in the master bedroom's closet.

Charlie "beat" the safe's code out of shorty and Prosper went to enter the numbers that he had already commenced to memory the night before. The shit was just brilliant. Anyone who watched the video footage wouldn't be the wiser.

Unfortunately, as soon as the cousins were headed out of the front door, a nigga Charlie assumed was her man came up from what had to be a soundproof basement with murder in his eyes.

The look in shorty's eyes told Charlie that she wasn't aware of his change in plans. Regrettably, her look also told her nigga that she was in on whatever betrayal she was currently participating in. Without a moment of hesitation, the fat dude produced a gun from seemingly thin air. One swift blast through her right eye socket ended not only her ability to see, but her ability to live.

The two cousins had never witnessed a murder before and was stuck on stupid as the woman's head permanently fell backwards at an odd angle. The crazy ass nigga had the nerve to smile at his handiwork before his attention was directed toward the terrified teenagers.

Luckily, moving targets were so much more difficult to hit than the sitting duck tied up to the chair. The man fired two shots, but luckily for the boys, he missed both times. His big ass surprised them with his speed.

The fat dude actually chased and kept up with the teens longer than they expected. When the shots resumed, their panic grew. The obese man's stamina had run its course, so he now had to rely on his gun to catch up to them. An act from God spared Charlie's life.

When the man released his final bullet, which was aligned perfectly with the back of Charlie's head, Charlie stumbled and fell mere seconds before the bullet reached his medulla oblongata. The bullet had been so close to hitting him that he literally felt the air from it breeze past him.

The fall was excruciating; however, it didn't hurt nearly as bad as a bullet to the skull did. As he laid face first on the pavement, he was certain that the gunman was going to kill him. He waited motionless for his ending to come. He didn't turn over because he didn't want to see it coming. He only prayed that his cousin kept running and saved himself. Someone had to live and make his now not so smart plan worth it.

After waiting and waiting for his life to be cut short, he realized that nothing was happening. As terrified as he was to investigate, he just had to know why the attack ceased. Did the guy assume that he was dead and just leave? Maybe the fast approaching sirens spooked him off. At any rate, Charlie had a decision to make.

He slowly sat up grimacing from not only the pain from the fall, but also from the realization that he had pissed on himself.

"Fuck!" He scalded himself.

While he was banged up and pissy, there was no sign of the fat nigga from down the street. Standing up as quickly as he could, he limped further down the street where he had parked his car. He didn't want to get caught up by the police. Charlie knew that he wasn't innocent in the situation.

After all, he had broken into a man's house and robbed him. How would he explain everything? A man has the right to protect his home, correct? With that in mind the decision was easy. He prayed that Prosper was there waiting for him.

"Damn it cuz!" Charlie hissed when he didn't see Prosper waiting for him by the car.

He went to the trunk and found a shirt and used it to protect his seat from his pissy pants as he got in. He watched the police, fire department and ambulance all come and go down the street. He waited for Prosper to show up for an agonizing six hours before he determined that he wasn't coming. He cried like a baby when he finally pulled off towards his home.

Charlie literally showered, got dressed and headed straight over to his cousin's house. He had a key, so he just let himself in. He was surprised to see his aunt in rare form. She was up watching the news. Normally she drank all night and slept all day. He told her that he thought Prosper was in trouble, but not the specifics of course.

They both placed calls to people they knew and told them to be on the lookout for him. Charlie must've called

Prosper's phone two hundred times without luck. This further heightened his anxiety. When Charlie saw Prosper walk through the door, that was perhaps the happiest moment of his life. So, when he saw his cousin break down, he understood that raw emotion. After giving Prosper time to compose himself, Charlie told Prosper to meet him on the porch.

Once outside the two cousins stood quietly for a moment while they both tried to figure out the best starting place for their conversation. So much had happened in the last twelve hours. They both thought each other were laying in a morgue somewhere.

Charlie decided to go first, followed by Prosper.

When they finished speaking, they gave each other manly hugs and vowed never to do anymore stupid shit like that again.

"Yeah man, that was some crazy gangsta movie shit. For real. I still feel bad for shorty back there man. She has two kids by that nigga. I see why she was fucking around on ole' dude. That nigga was fat as fuck and he is crazy. If he could murk the mother of his kids like that without hesitation, then no one else stood a chance. So, where's the money? I'm ready to do some spending after almost dying!" Charlie half joked.

While Charlie laughed at himself, Prosper suddenly felt lightheaded. In the midst of all of the mayhem, it dawned on him that he had left the bag containing the money, drugs and guns in the pretty shy girl's car. He was embarrassed to admit that he didn't know her name, although, he did notice her at school.

Slowly looking at his cousin, he defeatedly said, "Man, you might want to sit down for this."

# « Chapter 6 Nosy By Association »

"**MAN, ARE YOU FUCKING** serious?! Awww man! That bitch is probably at the police station right now turning us in! I mean, I know I always say that I would rather be judged by twelve than to be carried by six, but man I'm too pretty to go to prison. I bet the cops are at my crib right now interrogating my mom! Shit!" Charlie panicked.

Prosper was worried too and if the situation wasn't so fucked up, he'd be clowning his cousin's dramatic ass. Charlie was one of those pretty Jesse Williams types of dudes that truly wouldn't last in prison.

"Look cousin, she isn't a bitch. She's pretty dope actually, and she risked her safety helping me out. She doesn't seem like the snitching type. Hopefully, she won't even go through the bag and will bring it to school tomorrow. I won't let her out of my sight tomorrow until I get it, okay? Again, I'm so sorry for slipping like this." Prosper asserted.

Charlie was still heated, but he knew his cousin was a nigga of honor, so he trusted him when he said that he'd collect what was rightfully theirs from that bitch...young lady in his class.

Once Rae made it back home, she parked and nearly left Prosper's bag in her car, but she remembered just as she was closing the door. She damn near threw her back out because she wasn't expecting to lift as much weight as she had.

"What in the hell is in there? Rocks?!" She asked herself a loud.

"How in the hell was he just casually toting this thing around like it weighed nothing?" She continued talking to herself.

Normally, she wasn't the snooping, nosy type...who the hell are we kidding? Yes, she definitely was.

She cautiously opened the bag and received the shock of her life.

"Well there's definitely not rocks in here, but there's certainly some powder." She snapped.

She was furious that he would have that type of paraphernalia around her. She never thought of him to be a drug pusher. She was so disgusted and turned off because none of this was ever a part of her fantasies of him. There's nothing worse than finding out that superheroes are nothing more than mere mortals.

She couldn't even estimate how much money was in the bag. She counted ten bricks of cocaine. The feeling of hard metal piqued her interest. Once she got a good grip, she took it from its burial of coke and money. When the sight of the gun came into focus, she released a piercing scream. Guns were absolutely frightening to her. She instinctively wiped the pistol free of her fingerprints and replaced the gun just as Ant and Sam popped their heads out of the front door.

Walking over to their sister, they asked if everything was okay since they had heard her scream. She assured them that everything was okay as she reached for the bag.

Ant always needing to baby his sister swiftly took possession of the bag and said, "Little sis, let me get that for you."

Before she could protest, he had already grabbed it and was headed towards the house. Rae quickly set the alarm to her car and ran as fast as her thick legs would carry her. By the time she entered the threshold of their front door, Ant was already upstairs turning into her room. She prayed that he didn't peek into the bag like she had.

Unfortunately for her, nosiness ran in their blood. When she rounded the corner and entered her room, Ant was already separating the drugs, money, guns and the jewelry that she had overlooked. She stopped in her tracks trying to think of a logical explanation as to why she was carrying around a bag filled with enough illegal shit to receive twenty life sentences.

By the time her brother directed his attention to her, Rae's mouth was dry, and she suddenly had to shit. Her bowels were on fire, but she knew they'd have to wait.

Without saying a word to her, Ant walked towards her bedroom door and summoned Sam upstairs. Sam strolled in looking annoyed eating an oversized bowl of fruit loops. That is until his dark brown eyes landed on the mini fortune resting on Rae's bed. He quickly closed and locked the door behind him. He set his bowl of cereal down and Rae went and picked it up.

She wasn't hungry but she felt she needed a second last meal before they killed her.

Rae watched her brothers intently as they combed through the shit on her bed. Finally, Sam spoke up.

"Ummm sis, is there any logical reason as to why you are in possession of damn near a million dollars of cash, drugs, guns and hot ass jewelry?"

Rae recounted the entire story to her big brothers. She never lied to them, so she didn't feel the need to start that day. When her story came to an end, she noticed that Sam's poker face was on display as usual. Ant had always been much more transparent. He was furious and she could see it. He was dark just like Rae, but his reddish undertones were standing out since he was angry. Rae knew how the situation looked and she was more embarrassed than anything.

Sam looked more Puerto Rican than he did black and Dominican.

Ant was the first to speak up, "Desirae, I'm going to ask you this shit once, and you better not lie or I'm going to fuck you up and then call mom and pops in here. Do you understand?"

Rae glanced at Sam for a little assistance with their hot-tempered older brother, but through him, she received nothing more than a shrug of his shoulders.

Defeated, she poked her bottom lip out and nodded.

"Are you fucking now? Did you fuck that nigga last night?!" Ant spazzed.

Rae's eyes damn near bulged from their sockets. For a moment, she reflected on the story that she'd just told them, but for the life of her, she couldn't pinpoint any time where she'd given either of them the impression that she was sexing.

The look of rage on her brother's face snapped her out of her reflection and she quickly denied her brother's insinuation.

"No Ant! Come on now! You both know me better than that. I'd never disrespect this house or myself like that!" She snapped looking her brother straight in the eye.

Her reaction and passion told him all he needed to know. He knew his sister was being truthful.

Still upset Rae continued, "Furthermore, out of all the stuff that I just told you, you are upset about some shit that I didn't say????!!!"

"Alright little girl, I believe you but don't talk yourself into an ass whooping." Was Ant's way of apologizing.

He was forever threatening to beat her ass, yet she knew he'd never hurt her or allow anyone else to either.

"Alright, so here's what we are going to do..." Sam began.

"Hold up, what do you mean we? You two have nothing to do with any of this. This is my mess to clean up. I can handle it." Rae said.

"Are you finished or are you done? As I was saying, we aren't going to let you touch that coke. You can return that little nigga's money, jewelry and guns, but we are taking the coke. You can give him my number if he has any objections, though I have a strong feeling that he won't. You could've turned him in, so I'm certain that he'll be grateful to take whatever he gets.

For a lack of any other choice she simply asked, "But what are y'all going to do with all of that coke?"

The two men glanced at each other knowingly, but didn't entertain their naive sister with a response.

The next morning Desirae woke up early, mostly to avoid her parents. Her brothers had bid their farewells the night before and although she'd never admit it, she missed their annoying asses already. She was nervous all the way to school because she feared getting pulled over with the contents of the bag tucked away in her trunk.

She drove slower than an old woman on a Sunday morning. Their school had metal detectors, so she knew that she'd have to catch Prosper before he entered the school. What he did with the bag after that was his problem.

Prosper was a nervous wreck. He didn't think that the cute girl from school would throw him under the bus, but he couldn't be too sure. After all, he knew absolutely nothing about her.

After dropping Serena off over at Charlie's house, he made his way to school. His heart leaped up into his throat when he spotted the girl's glittery car in the student parking lot. She must've spotted him too, because she quickly got out and went to her trunk.

A wave of relief washed over him once he noticed that she was carrying the bag that he'd promised his cousin that he'd get today. Prosper walked over towards her and she handed the bag over to him. He immediately noticed that the weight was off.

Noticing his confused expression Rae stated, "My brothers kept the dope. His number is in the bag if you have any questions."

With that, Rae walked towards the school with no intentions on ever speaking to the sexy boy ever again.

## « Chapter 7 Invisible »

**RAE CRIED INCONSOLABLY** as she hugged her family prior to boarding the plane that would transport her to her future. For the first time in her life, she was all on her own...well in a way. Zo had applied and gotten accepted to Maryville University in Missouri as well. He was majoring in history. They both received full rides for being exceptional academically.

His ability to remember people and events was amazing. During Rae's first couple of months away from home she regretted her decision to go to school so far away from her family. Between her and Zo's hectic schedules, the two of them rarely had the opportunity to see each other, although, they did manage to talk and FaceTime most days.

Rae had taken on an extremely heavy load at school and against her advisor's wishes, she enrolled into eighteen credit hours her very first semester at Maryville. She had always excelled easily in high school, but college was a different ballgame. Especially considering she was a premed student.

She had to conjure up the discipline it took to maintain her focus in order to survive her first semester. She moved around campus robotically as if she were invisible. No one really noticed her, and she liked it that way. As she lost herself in the hustle and bustle of campus life, she couldn't help but to notice that she was putting on even more weight.

She had heard of the freshman fifteen, however she had surpassed that by twenty pounds. Her clothing was becoming snugger and her self-esteem further face planted. Zo did all that he could to lift his best friend's spirit up, but his attempts proved futile.

Rae felt that she should've listened to her parents and attended a university back home. She thought that by going to college in another state, that it would somehow erase her unpleasant high school experience.

Sometimes when her mind relaxed a little, thoughts of Prosper took over. She often wondered how he was and if he was happy. After she gave him back his bag of illegal shit, she literally tried to delete him from her memory bank. The roles had somewhat reversed. She now caught him staring at her at school and he made no effort to hide it.

He liked what he saw, and he wanted her to know it. Despite his deep attraction to the plus sized beauty, Prosper knew that publicly showing his attraction to her wasn't the popping thing to do. Hell, now that he had come up on that lick, bitches were throwing pussy at him left and right.

Nevertheless, life went on and high school eventually had to come to an end. She always felt so silly whenever she thought about him, because she was certain that he was living his best life back home and not concerning himself with her.

She was not friends with him on social media, however since his pages were public, she was able to lurk around and keep tabs on him discreetly. Rae had read that he had remained close to home and had opted to attend Texas A&M University.

Ironically, he majored in criminal justice. It seemed like such a serious profession for such a seemingly law-breaking guy. Rae had no idea that he was interested in criminology, however, she really didn't know much about him at all.

Seeing his smiling face on social media always made Rae miss home even more. She had noticed that one of their old classmates named Claryssa frequently made guest appearances on his pages. It wasn't long at all before Prosper's relationship status changed from single to in a relationship.

Who knew that something so trivial could be so utterly devastating? That status update had nearly caused Rae to fail her anatomy and physiology midterm exam. Claryssa was the total package, at least physically anyway in Rae's eyes.

While anyone could see that Rae had a more aesthetically pleasing face, Claryssa had the perfect "slim thick" hourglass figure. Claryssa was also a redbone with bundles fraudulently cascading down her back. Rae knew that for most guys, especially college students, a banging body was typically the most important attribute a woman could have.

Rae knew that her chances, however slim of ever getting with Prosper were officially dead now that he was with Claryssa. Why would he want someone like her when he had Claryssa on his arm?

After some time and verbal lashings from Zo, Rae eventually grew to accept that she and Prosper would never be. Rae had somehow managed to have her room to herself during her first semester, however, as the semester concluded, she was informed that she would be getting a roommate who was a second-year student whose dorm had flooded. That's when things started to get a little interesting.

When Whisper Jones entered the small dorm room for the first time, Rae wasn't sure what to think. Whisper was certainly a colorful character. She was from the Bronx and was a little on the ghetto side. She was loud, opinionated, and abrasive. She was brown skin and cute, but in a rachet sort of way.

She sported insanely long coffin shaped nails and had five different colors in her waist length braids. Like most people, her outspoken personality was the polar opposite of Rae's. It wasn't until Whisper lifted her cheek length false lashes that Rae noticed the girl had the prettiest two toned greenish-hazel eyes.

Whisper came in and immediately said, "Look, I'm not into drama. I'll respect you, if you respect me. I don't like a lot of muthafuckas in my space. If you or your company steal my shit, *you* will replace it. Ask before borrowing or eating my shit. I don't eat pussy, so don't try me. Oh, and my name is Whisper Jones."

Unfazed, Rae simply looked up at the colorful girl, shrugged her shoulders and went back to reading her textbook without a word.

From Whisper's bold speech she sounded like the perfect roommate, Rae just didn't particularly care for her brazen approach. She was the newcomer coming in trying to call the shots and that rubbed Rae the wrong way a little bit. She had decided that the two of them would just cohabitate the same space, but that didn't mean that they had to get along or be friends.

In fact, Rae wanted nothing to do with the little rude

heifer. Their little living arrangement worked well for months. They both came and went only speaking to each other when they had to. Rae never had any drama because she didn't know anyone besides Zo. When the two of them got together it was typically for lunch or in his dorm room. Zo's roommate was rarely there, so they could have a good time without disturbing anyone.

Zo was having the time of his life. He was really enjoying Missouri and told Rae that he wasn't sure if he would be returning to Texas after they finished school. He was dating a little, but nothing too serious. He was always trying to convince Rae to go out and mingle with other likewise single people, but she was just way too awkward.

She had actually convinced herself that no one would want to be with someone her size. Rae had never even gone out on a date before. Out of her and her two best friends, the only one who had been asked to prom in high school was Afrika, however, she turned the boy down and they went as a trio. They looked really nice too.

The closest that she had ever been to a boy was when Prosper was about to kiss her before his ignorant ass friends had interrupted them...also when he had caressed her face in her bed.

It was amazing how that one isolated display of affection had her smitten by him. If she closed her eyes and concentrated hard enough, she could almost feel his touch still lingering on her skin. That was now a distant memory because he had moved on.

"Sis, I am so serious! You need to get your pretty ass out there and find you a man. I'm not saying that you have to marry them, but live your life hun. This is the time when you should be out here dating and experiencing different people. Promise me that you will at least try to enjoy yourself a little while we are here.

We are far away from our parents and should be creating memories that will last us for the rest of our lives. I know how important your studies are to you, but you cannot be all work without playing a little." Zo said.

He wasn't wrong...

## « Chapter 8 Check Please »

"HELLO, I'M DESIRAE AND you must be Darnell?" Rae bashfully introduced herself to the handsome guy standing next to a white BMW.

After ten months of going from her dorm room to her classes on campus, Rae had finally decided to listen to her bestie and go out on a date. She had almost cancelled at least a half a dozen times due to her nerves.

"Wow, you are even prettier than your profile picture. How did I get so lucky?" Darnell countered genuinely while placing a soft kiss on top of her right hand.

Rae blushed at the gesture. She then allowed her hazel eyes to rake over Darnell's appearance. He was dressed nicely without being overly flashy. He was outfitted in a nice button up shirt and a nice pair of slacks.

He was about five foot ten inches with a slight muscular build. He was light skin with a fresh fade and a clean-shaven face that made him appear more youthful than he actually was. To make matters even better, Darnell was very polite and extremely well-spoken.

Rae herself was clad in a pink form fitting dress that Zo had picked out for her. The girdle that she sported underneath made it nearly impossible to breathe comfortably. She donned cute white sandals that she found on sale on the Gucci website and a cute cardigan to further hide her insecurities.

She'd straightened her hair to perfection which she rarely had the patience to do often. Not being a huge fan of makeup, she opted for a little mascara and pink lipstick to complete her look. She looked amazing, yet her weight wouldn't allow her to see it.

Her date certainly took notice as he trailed behind her to the restaurant before he stepped up and opened the door for her. He licked his lips as her sweet scent caressed his olfactory system. She was certainly much bigger than what he was used to, but at least she was shapely with it. She wasn't sloppy fat. Plus, she knew how to dress her weight. That was the issue with a lot of big girls. They assume less means more.

After the two were seated, they awkwardly stared down at their menus. Their nervousness was kind of cute actually. Looking over the menu, Rae suddenly felt conflicted. She was starving and wanted to order several items on the menu, yet she didn't want to turn her date off either.

After going back and forth between the tantalizing pages, she'd compromised by ordering a steak with a baked potato and asparagus. Although she liked the strawberry lemonade at that particular restaurant, she didn't want to come off as too high maintenance, so she settled for a glass of water with lemons. If she were still hungry after they had eaten dinner, she could always pick something up after the date ended.

When it came time for Darnell to order, Rae almost regretted not ordering more food. His greedy ass ordered two appetizers, the steak and seafood platter and a glass of her favorite strawberry lemonade...which was refilled twice, and they weren't free. Let's not forget the caramel cheesecake that he ordered for dessert.

Despite his ravenous appetite, they both eventually opened up and the conversation began to flow effortlessly. Darnell was also a freshman in college and was majoring in communications. He was born and raised in St. Louis in a two-parent household, which Rae loved. Family was so important to her.

She realized that they had quite a bit in common and had already began to make plans to see him again in the near future. She told Darnell about herself as well as her plans for the future.

Before they knew it, hours had passed, and their waitress was starting to walk by more frequently as if silently reminding them to get the hell out. Rae eventually waved her over and told her that they were ready for the check. The young waitress looked relieved and briskly walked away to get their check.

Not wanting the night to end, the two continued talking and enjoying themselves. The waitress finally returned with their check enclosed inside of a black server book. Neither Rae nor Darnell reached for the book, so the confused waitress slowly lowered it in the middle of the table and walked away.

After a few moments, Rae curiously reached for the book. She was a little annoyed, but figured that since it was their first date, she wouldn't trip about going Dutch. She was cool with paying for her food. Her eyes bulged out of their sockets when she saw the total price of the bill was one hundred three dollars minus the suggested tip for the waitress.

Rae estimated her portion to be thirty dollars including taxes and her portion for the tip. She opened up her purse and peeled off the money. She then closed and slid the book over to Darnell. He reluctantly opened the book. She noted the familiar bulging of his eyes before reaching into his pocket for his wallet. Inwardly she laughed. After all, what did his little greedy ass expect?

Her petty thoughts were short lived once she noted the look of panic take over his handsome face.

Clearing her throat, she softly asked, "Is everything okay?"

Surely, he wasn't about to hit her with the classic "I forgot my wallet at home" was he?

Continuing to pat his pancake flat pockets, Darnell replied, "Desirae, I don't know quite how to say this, but I seem to have forgotten my wallet at home. I'm so embarrassed. Do you think that you can just cover for the both of us and I can wire you the money when I get home?"

The common sense in Rae was telling her to request separate bills and to hightail it out of there, yet the compassionate part of her allowed a weak "okay" to escape her lips. Rae dejectedly picked up the money that she had previously put into the book.

She then returned them back into her wallet. She found her emergency credit card and put it into the book instead. She knew her parents were going to give her a tongue lashing later about frivolously spending over a hundred dollars on a meal. Once again, she waved the waitress over.

As the waitress busied herself with charging Rae's card, Darnell continued to apologize and made promises to pay her back. By this time Rae had already left the date mentally, she was just stuck there physically. She couldn't believe how quickly the date had gone wrong.

He seemed to have it going on initially, but couldn't even pay for his portion of the bill. She was so turned off. Everything that was attractive about him, suddenly wasn't anymore. She just wanted it to end already.

Rae wasn't even in the mood to remain cordial to Darnell's broke ass at this point. As far as she was concerned, this was the very last time she'd ever be seeing his broke ass. As soon as she received her card back, she stood up and switched her plump ass out of the restaurant without looking back.

As she got situated in her seat and was applying her seatbelt, she sucked her teeth when she heard a light tap on her driver's window. Reluctantly she rolled her window down a half an inch. After all, she didn't know his ass and the few facts that she thought that she knew were all questionable as well.

Without saying a word to Darnell, she questioningly raised her arched eyebrows as if to say what the hell do you want now. Getting the hint, Darnell began to stutter as he dropped yet another bombshell.

"Ummmm Desirae. I am so sorry about all this..."

Cutting him off she countered, "I already know Darnell. You've apologized already. We are good. Goodnight!"

Scanning the parking lot and not seeing the white BMW she asked, "Where's your car? You know what? It's none of my business. I don't even care."

As she went to roll her window up on his ass, he yelled out, "Please wait! I'm only sixteen...well I'll be seventeen next week. My pops isn't answering his phone and I really need a ride home. Please don't leave me here."

The world as Rae knew it seemed to stop for a moment as the enormity of Darnell's words sank in.

"Sixteen?! You're fucking sixteen!!! Oh my God! Are you trying to get me sent to prison?!"

Rae who was typically very reserved chewed his young ass out for a solid five minutes before allowing him into her car. She typed his address into her GPS and turned her music up loud so that he wouldn't be tempted to speak to her. Once she reached his house, she kept her gaze straight ahead.

She could feel his eyes burning a hole into the side of her face, but refused to entertain him any further. She had wasted enough time on that little boy. Once her passenger door closed, she sped off without so much as a glance in her rearview mirror.

## « Chapter 9 What's Your Status »

"**THAT'S RIGHT Y'ALL.** Laugh it on up. I hope both of you choke! That was one of the worse experiences of my life and you bastards are making jokes about it!" Rae huffed in frustration.

Maybe in time she'd find the situation as humorous as Afrika and Zo, but today her voice cracked through the phone as she recounted her date from hell. Rae was over at Zo's place and they had Afrika on speaker.

"Well didn't you say that he did actually pay you back the next day?" Zo asked knowingly.

"Yes, he did pay it back with interest. He texted me this long message about how he really liked me and hoped that I could find it in my heart to forgive him. Oh, and he reminded me that he will be eighteen in a year." Rae groaned.

"What did you say to his message?" Afrika asked giggling again.

"Not a damn thing. I blocked and then deleted his number. I then blocked him from the dating app. I'm not trying to end up on the sex offender registry!" Rae snapped.

"Girl, calm all that shit down. The boy is about to be seventeen and you're just nineteen. Nothing wrong with that. Give him some credit." Zo stated seriously.

"Let's just talk about something else." Afrika suggested playing the mediator.

∞

After splitting the money from the heist and getting rid of the guns and jewelry, both Prosper and Charlie ended up with enough money to jumpstart any dream that they ever felt was impossible. Naturally, Charlie was pissed about Rae's brothers keeping the coke, but Prosper was able to remind him that the brothers could've kept everything and not sent shit back. The coke was never meant for them anyway.

Charlie had always wanted to open up a soul food restaurant and so he made that shit happen. He loved to cook and now he could rake in cash doing what he loved. He named his restaurant Avery's Soul Food after he and Prosper's late grandmother.

After all, most of his recipes were in fact hers that she had shared. Opening up a business...especially a food-based business came with its fair share of setbacks and headaches, however, when he finally opened up for business it was all worth it.

Prosper actually tried his hand in the real estate game. He'd always admired the successes that his former stepfather had with his real estate dealings. His first investment was a little cheap run-down house that he rehabbed for the low and was able to triple his profits.

By the time he completed his first year of college, he had finally opened up a real estate office and he had started purchasing more expensive houses and was rewarded with even larger profits. The cousins were certainly winning. He had even switched his major to business.

Perhaps the biggest victory was getting both Shawn and Dawn into rehabilitation facilities to assist them with their alcoholism. Both sisters relapsed and enabled one another, but after six months of playing tug of war, both were sober, healthy and happy. For the first time in Serena's short life, Prosper began to take on more of a brotherly role as he permitted Shawn to take the wheel. He had slowly transitioned into and embraced his college life.

Prosper had even put a title on the chick who he'd been seeing in high school. He had resisted because he knew deep down, he wasn't ready. He was young and horny and not ready to be tied down to one female, however the plus sign that appeared on the third positive pregnancy test made him put his selfish desires aside and man up. He cheated on Claryssa and he cheated a little more. He wasn't trying to hurt her, but temptation was a muthafucka.

By the time their daughter Bobbie was born, he had decided that he was officially done running around. Bobbie was named after Claryssa's brother who had drowned when they were kids. Looking at his daughter made him regret every tear he had caused Claryssa to shed. He'd kill a nigga for even thinking about exposing his daughter to that level of pain.

Not that he didn't respect women before, but after having a daughter gave Prosper a whole new prospective on them. Claryssa may not have been exactly who he had planned to settle down with, but for the sake of his daughter, he was determined to make it work.

When he asked Claryssa to marry him, he had no doubt in his mind that she would say yes. Of course, she didn't disappoint him. Prosper gave her a choice, they could have a courthouse wedding immediately or they could wait and have a ceremony after he graduated.

Claryssa opted to get married immediately and so that's what they did. The only people who were present were Claryssa's parents, Shawn, Serena, Charlie and of course Bobbie. It wasn't anything fancy, but Prosper's heart was in the right place. He wanted to do right by the mother of his child.

He just hated that school wouldn't allow him time to have an actual ceremony and honeymoon. He planned to surprise her later. He'd give her the honeymoon and wedding that she deserved for sticking with him even when he didn't deserve it.

Back in Missouri, a blurry eyed Rae cried as she had just read Prosper's relationship status updated once again to 'Married'.

## « Chapter 10 More Than A Whisper »

"FUCK IT!" A CONFLICTED Whisper mumbled to herself as she crossed over the imaginary barrier and onto her roommate's side of the room.

She typically didn't make it her business to be up in other people's business, yet she couldn't bear to watch the woman who she shared her living space with to continue to lay in bed and cry all day.

"Desirae? Desirae...are you okay? What's up with you lately?" Whisper asked showing Rae more compassion and conversing more than she had since moving in.

"Nothing, I'll be alright." Rae forced out miserably.

"Look, I know that I don't know you like that, but it's amazing how much you pick up on after living with someone. With that being said, I know you're not alright. You are experiencing the type of pain that only a fuckboy can bring about. You should know by now that the best victory is to succeed.

You're a gorgeous woman and the sad part is I can tell that you don't even know it. And that humility probably makes you even more attractive. I can tell by your lack of confidence in the clothes you wear and simply by observing your body language. Yes, you are a big girl and that's alright, but I can see that it affects you. You may not have noticed, but I am a personal trainer.

I am double majoring in nutrition and physical therapy. So, if you are serious about this...I'm willing to help you out. Those little temporary diets that I've seen you trying aren't going to work for you. We need to overhaul your entire lifestyle. Plus, that sneaky ass closet eating would have to stop. You can't hide from or fool the scale.

Fair warning, it will not be easy. I'm tough, but if you stick it out and listen to me, I promise you that I'll turn you into a ten. Trust the process sis!"

Finally removing her plush lavender comforter from over her head Rae asked, "Can I think about it for a few days?"

"Of course, take all the time you need, but let me know by Friday." Whisper stated seriously, while Rae cracked a smile at the contradictory laced comment.

Zo had finally found the courage to not only learn how to drive, but he had also recently purchased his first car. Rae was so proud of her friend. It was nice to have him pick her up and chauffeur her around for a change.

Rae had selected a cute black one-piece body suit with red five-inch heels. Her girdle had managed to squish in most of her unsightly rolls while her trusted cardigan masked the rest. She took the time that evening to do her makeup, but she kept her hair in its naturally curly state. Her red Prada clutch completed her look.

"Bitch! If I didn't like this bussy getting beat up from time to time I'd marry yo fine ass!" Her friend complimented in his vulgar way.

"Thanks boo. You don't look bad yourself." Rae admitted.

Rae loved wearing white because he said that it just looked clean and royal...whatever the hell that meant. He wore white distressed skinny jeans with a white Gucci shirt. She really admired his all white high-top Jordan's and white Gucci belt. She couldn't help but to roll her eyes when he pulled out white framed Gucci glasses to complete his look. He'd cut his hair into a curly Mohawk and the style suited him well.

"Alright heifer, I'm gonna need you to remove the thirst from your eyes when you look at me. I'm gay, but don't think I can't perform with a female as well! I'm ambidextrous when I need to be!" His goofy ass joked.

"Zo, ambidextrous refers to the ability to use your right and left hand equally...the term you're looking for is bisexual and let me find out..." Rae teased her friend.

"Oh yeah, well in that case I am ambidextrous too!" His nasty ass admitted.

"Ewww! TMI! Anyway, where in the hell are you taking us? I don't even feel like going out for real." Rae said.

"Well, that's just too damn bad. You've been hiding in that damn room long enough. No more avoidance. I've known you practically my whole life, you don't always have to be strong around me." Zo stated.

"I know and I'm sorry for shutting you out. It won't happen again. I know you've got my back." She said.

"I got your front too, bitch." Zo laughed as he playfully cupped Rae's pussy before taking off running. Running behind him, she chased his ass all the way to his car and mushed him when she made it.

Zo took them to a new night club called Eddie's. Night clubs really weren't her scene, however, she just wanted to unwind and take her classes and Prosper off of her mind for a while. Zo almost immediately disappeared onto the dance floor. Rae had to decline the alcohol and opted to sip on Sprite at the bar.

"Keep em coming!" Rae yelled to the bartender mimicking the alcoholics chugging down shots.

Seven Rings by Ariana Grande began to play, which was currently Rae's shit. She didn't have the guts to get up and dance, however, she gyrated and grinded the hell out of her bar stool. A light tap on her left shoulder brought her out of her musical trance.

She slowly turned around to see who had interrupted her and immediately grew annoyed. The homely looking dude immediately turned her off. He was high yellow and had huge craters plastered all over his face.

His uneven gapped teeth were heavily coated in plaque which instantly turned Rae's stomach. Being a future dentist, healthy teeth and pretty smiles were everything. Homeboy's gingivitis was so bad that his gums were bleeding from simply smiling at her.

She was all for supporting the beard gang, however that pussy hair faced dude was just grotesque!

"Good evening beautiful, my name is Larry. What's your name?" He inquired attempting to place his chapped lips on top of her hand, but she hurriedly snatched it away.

Rae decided to be polite and let him down gently. She didn't want any smoke with that guy.

Instead she smiled and said, "Hi there Larry. My name is Shameeka. I'm actually here with my boyfriend tonight...sorry."

She felt that her rejection was polite, concise and clear.

Larry, who apparently was fed up with the constant rejection retorted, "Well, fuck you too then, you fat bitch!"

Had the insult come from anyone else it might've stung a little, but she just couldn't find it within herself to be bothered by the Crypt Keeper.

Shrugging it off, her "fat ass" ordered another Sprite.

Over the next hour and a half Rae turned away a few more guys before a perspiring Zo found her and asked if she were ready to leave.

"Duh!!! I was ready to go before we even got here! You should've seen Jerome from the show Martin trying to holler at me!" She cackled.

Zo simply shook his head and led his picky friend out of the club.

Once they had almost reached his car, Rae whined, "I got to pee!"

"Bitch! Why didn't you just pee inside the club? You're screwed now because once you leave, there is no reentry." Zo scolded his friend.

The back to back Sprites were finally catching up to Rae. She stood there trying to weigh her options. She could piss outside and use some of the tissues that were in her purse. However, getting her snug one-piece body suit off was going to be difficult. Why in the hell had she worn that shit anyway?! The second option was for her to attempt to make it to a nearby gas station or restaurant. Just when she'd decided on the latter option, that fool, Larry walked up to her and Zo.

"So, you mean to tell me that your boyfriend is a sissy? You bitches kill me!"

Zo went to swing on Larry for disrespecting his friend, but Larry swiftly produced a shiny pistol that stopped him dead in his tracks. Rae on the other hand didn't need to find a restroom any longer, because her bladder had just involuntarily emptied itself.

"Man, what the fuck did your punk ass think that you were about to do sissy? I should shoot your ass for even thinking about swinging on me!" Larry fumed and raised the gun to Zo.

Zo remained stoic, but Rae could see his jaw muscles flexing which meant that he was infuriated. Zo may have been gay, but he was nobody's bitch. He'd had his fair share of fights over the years related to his sexual preferences and he'd easily won ninety-five percent of them.

Knowing her stubborn friend would die before submitting to Larry, Rae pleaded, "Look Larry, please put the gun down. He didn't mean to come at you that way. Can we please leave now?"

After a few moments Larry actually complied by lowering the gun. He then walked over to Rae. He stood so close that Rae could tell that Larry had consumed chitterlings at some point that day...or at least it smelled like it.

"Pissy, go and take sissy and get the fuck out of here before I change my mind! Hurry the fuck up bitches!" Larry clowned, dispersing droplets of his spittle onto Rae's lips.

Larry walked away, but not before kindly relieving Zo of his Rolex watch that he had received as a graduation present.

## « Chapter 11 Love At First Swipe »

"OHHHHH RAE! WHAT about him?!" Zo squealed.

Not expecting much, Rae reluctantly looked over his shoulder and at the screen. After her first disastrous date, she was terrified of stepping out with another potential train wreck, Rae's jaw literally dropped once her eyes focused on the gorgeous guy.

He looked like a young Gary Dourdan...green eyes and honey blonde dreads and all. After reading his lengthy profile, she was convinced that she was in love with that man and words hadn't even been exchanged yet.

"Unh hunh. Just like I thought." Her bestie chuckled while swiping right.

"Well, will ya look at that? You're a match!" He squealed again.

"Send him a message for me please and hurry up before someone else snatches up that scccchhhnack!" Rae's corny ass attempted to sound cool.

Later that day Rae began to communicate with the handsome stranger. They hit it off so well that they eventually exchanged real names and numbers. Rae thought that he was lying when he told her that his name was Martin.

He didn't look like a Martin at all, but he explained that his grandmother adored the late great Dr. Martin Luther King Jr and wanted her first and only grandson to live up to such a name. Martin was a tattoo artist and was twenty-five, which intimidated Rae just a little bit.

She prayed that he would find her attractive. She was honest about having a few extra pounds on her profile, but like most people unhappy with their bodies, she only posted cute selfies on the site.

 She just couldn't stomach putting a full body picture on display. She did feel somewhat deceptive. Based on her selfies, men constantly swiped right to her pictures, but would their fingers switch directions had she posted body pictures?

They conversed for hours and hit it off so well that he invited her to the tattoo party that he was hosting the following evening. He told her that he'd pick her up at seven. Before she could agree, she decided to disclose her waistline status.

"Ummm Martin. Before I agree to go, there is something that I need to tell you." Rae said dreadfully.

Her weight was truly becoming an embarrassing burden. It was almost as if she was about to disclose a positive HIV status.

"Damn. You got me nervous over here. You don't have AIDS over there do you?" He asked half-jokingly.

"Oh no...nothing like that at all. It's just that I ummm...I'm a big girl." She forced out.

She held her breath and closed her eyes bracing herself for what was to come.

"Big girl? I mean...like how big? My 600-lb Life big or Raven Symone big?" He asked in a serious tone.

Her mouth became super dry.

Her heart dropped to her rectum as tears filled her eyes. Just as she went to hang up the phone, she heard laughing coming from the receiver.

"Hello? Rae?" Martin asked worriedly.

"Yes?" She whispered.

"I'm sorry that I upset you. I was only joking. You're beautiful. I don't care about any of that shit. I thought you were about to tell me something terrible. Now will you agree to hang out tomorrow?" He inquired.

Wiping the tears that had managed to escape, Rae finally agreed, and their date was set.

The next day Rae tore through her closet trying to find the perfect outfit. Every outfit that she tried on only seemed to make her feel fatter than the last. She couldn't go out with Martin's fine ass looking the way she did.

Whisper sat on her bed quietly watching Rae damn near have a meltdown. She felt for her, yet didn't want to overstep her boundaries. It was difficult living with another female, especially one that you didn't know, but so far, they had been managing just fine. Whisper didn't want to rock the boat, yet something was compelling her to help the girl.

Walking over towards Rae's closet space, Whisper turned and asked, "May I?"

Rae sadly nodded and Whisper immediately went to work.

"Where are you going on your date? I mean like what kind of setting is it?" Whisper inquired so that she'd select an appropriate outfit for the setting.

"Ummm, I think it's going to be a tattoo party at the tattoo parlor, so I shouldn't get too dressed up right?" Rae asked nervously.

"I agree. You'll probably just be sitting for most of the time, so you want to be comfortable." Said Whisper.

Within five minutes Whisper had managed to find Rae the perfect outfit for her date with Martin. Rae had to give the girl credit; she had an eye for fashion. She felt bad for thinking that Whisper was just some ghetto hoodrat when she'd initially met her. She was the exact opposite...she just didn't tolerate any bullshit.

Rae opted to straighten her hair, hoping that it gave her rounded cheeks a slimmer look. By the time seven rolled around, Rae's stomach was in knots. She almost had a heart attack when Martin texted her stating that he was outside. She took some deep breaths and told herself that it was too late to back out.

Before walking out of her room, she looked at Whisper and said, "I truly appreciate you being here for me this past week. I've been going through some things and you have been a

Godsend. Although I'm a day late, I would love it if you could be my personal trainer...I mean if the offer still stands, of course."

Whisper pursed her glossed lips together and stared at Rae before saying, "I will train you, but this shit is serious business. You've got to want this shit more than I want it for you. You will follow my meal plan; you will work out every day with the exception of Sundays. If I feel that my time is being wasted, I will stop. I'd stop for a paying client so please know that I will axe your ass faster..."

"Okay, okay...I got it." Rae chuckled.

"I'm truly ready. I'm sure of it." Rae committed.

"Okay then. Since tomorrow is Sunday, we will just start fresh on Monday. By the time you come home, I'll have your meal plan ready. We will get your starting weight on Monday. Now you've kept your date waiting for you long enough, go and enjoy yourself." Whisper said.

Smiling from ear to ear, Rae thanked Whisper again and headed down to meet and greet her date.

Martin was already standing next to his car when Rae exited her building. She felt so self-conscious as he literally watched her walk the entire time. She felt as if she was walking funny under his intense gaze. He had dark sunglasses on, so she hoped that he liked what he saw. It was a little difficult to read him without seeing his eyes.

Once she reached him, he dismissed her handshake and bent down to give her a hug.

"Sup gorgeous? We are huggers where I'm from. Handshakes should be reserved for business purposes. Hugs are personal and all love. Feel me?" Martin informed her.

She wasn't exactly fond of the idea of hugging strangers,

but he was so sexy and smelled so good that he actually had to clear his throat to remind her to let go.

"I'm sorry about that." A mortified Rae blushed.

"It's all good shorty. I didn't want to let go either...trust."

When they arrived at the tattoo parlor, Rae noticed that there were probably one hundred cars parked in front, on the sides and most likely in the rear of the building as well.

Martin opened the passenger door to assist her out of his all black 2017 Lexus. She felt like a princess that evening. Although Martin was working, he still managed to cater to her throughout the evening.

When she wasn't watching Martin tatting customers up, she hung out with the receptionist, Christina or the twins KD and JD who were the piercers. Jimmy, the owner, ordered pizzas and wings for all of the employees as well as for Rae. Since she knew that her bootcamp would be starting soon, she took advantage of the hospitality.

Although their date wasn't exactly a traditional one, she couldn't think of a better one. Everyone made her feel right at home. The party didn't end until just before midnight, yet Rae was a little disappointed to be leaving.

"Well, it seems as if everyone adores you here." Martin observed.

"I really liked them too. They are cool people. I'd like to see them again." She admitted.

Martin smiled and wrapped his arm around her waist as he led her to his car.

Once they got in, he turned to Rae and said, "You know, I

feel really bad that I wasn't able to spend as much time with you as I would've liked. How do you feel about coming to hang out with me at my house? I mean nothing special...just a good movie and some snacks. If you aren't comfortable, I'll completely understand and take you home."

Without giving his proposition much thought, she quickly told him yes. He gave her a winning smile and interlocked her fingers with his as he drove off in the direction of his house.

When they arrived at Martin's house, Rae noticed that he didn't live in the greatest part of town, however she felt safe with him.

The house was small and old, but he kept it tidy. Rae was led to Martin's bedroom and browsed through movies on his jailbroken Firestick for a good comedy. They both agreed to watch Life. They ate popcorn and sipped on soda as they watched the classic.

At some point Martin pulled Rae over until she straddled his lap. Her body instantly froze up. In her mind she knew that she should probably leave, but feeling his erection poking at the thin material of her now dampened panties made her forget that she had a brain.

Martin started to thrust upwards while both hands grabbed her ass cheeks and guided her to grind on him while matching his rhythm. Who knew that something so limiting could feel so amazing? By the time her brain resurfaced, her dress had managed to disappear, as did her bra. The only remaining articles were her panties and girdle.

Embarrassed, she quickly hopped off of Martin and covered her breasts with her hands.

# « Chapter 12 Expired Plates »

"**MOVE YOUR HANDS.** I want to see everything. You're beautiful." Martin whispered removing Rae's hands from hiding her naked body.

She wanted to crawl into a hole and die due to the way that he was carefully scrutinizing her body. She squirmed under his watchful eyes, praying that he'd stop looking.

Rae lost her breath when his lips crushed her own. She had never been kissed before and electricity was tingling from places she never knew existed.

She was so engrossed in her first kiss that she didn't even feel Martin remove her panties. Before she could protest, she was swiftly lowered to her back. She was a big girl, but Martin moved her effortlessly.

She couldn't help but to wonder if she was dreaming. Was she about to lose her virginity to this guy that she barely knew? She never said that she would wait for marriage or anything, but she thought she'd lose her virginity under better circumstances for sure.

Rae couldn't even get her thoughts together before she felt her pussy being split into two. There was no foreplay or anything. She didn't even get to see what he was working with, but she sure felt it. She wanted to stop him. She didn't realize that she didn't want to have sex with him until after he was already stroking away. It was too late to stop by then...wasn't it?

Martin complimented Rae on how tight and good her virgin pussy was. He sounded as if he was thoroughly enjoying himself. She didn't have the heart to take that experience away from him, even if it meant giving a piece of herself up in the process.

Rae just accepted that she was going to give herself to Martin. She closed her eyes and cried out in pain as Martin roughly tore away at her hymen.

She almost rejoiced out loud when his body stiffened and convulsed on top of her. It wasn't until he withdrew himself from her center that she realized that he didn't bother to use any protection.

Rae decided that she was in way too much pain and was too tired to worry herself with such matters in that moment. She decided to get under the covers and take a nap.

Just as she got situated under the covers, she heard, "What are you doing? Get up. I never let bitches stay over. You

THE WHORE NEXT DOOR

got to bounce. Come on, I'll drop you off. With the good cat you just threw my way…it's the least a nigga can do."

"Bitches?" Rae questioned.

"Come on now. Don't go getting all sensitive and shit. You're not completely innocent. I just met you today and you already gave me the ass. Don't get me wrong, you are beautiful as fuck and I know you ain't no hoe or nothing, but I just can't wife up no fat bitch.

I toyed with the idea throughout the day, but I just can't. Now whenever you want to fuck, I'm your nigga, but that's all I can offer you right now. Now, if you slim down, I'd definitely cuff you." Martin elaborated breaking Rae's spirit.

Without another word she slowly got dressed and followed him to his car. He lived thirty minutes from her dorm. He tried to make casual small talk as if he didn't just stomp all over her fragile heart. It took everything in her not to break down in front of him, but she'd never give him the satisfaction.

Once they made it approximately five minutes from her dorm, red and blue lights began to flash behind them. Rae was relaxed because she knew that she didn't have anything to hide. Martin on the other hand immediately began to panic.

"Fuck! I got a fucking warrant! Damn, I'm going to jail. Shit! Listen Desirae, I really need you to have a nigga's back with this situation. I'm definitely about to get locked up. Can you hold me down and get me out? It's not a major charge or anything so it should be fairly cheap to get me out. Please, I'll pay you back every red cent. Plus...listen to this...I'll wife you up. I take back everything I just said. Please help me." Martin pleaded.

Rae just looked through him and thought of ways that she could murder him and not get caught.  To top it all off, she realized for the first time that his lying ass had dark brown eyes...not green ones as advertised. She had to give it to him. He had played her so well. Hell, he'd played her right out of some coochie.

The older cop cautiously approached the vehicle. He explained that he had pulled them over due to the expired plates. Just as Martin had predicted, they locked his ass up and towed away his vehicle. As bad as Rae didn't want to, she decided to just walk the rest of the way to her dorm room leaving a trail of tears along the way.

## « Chapter 13 The Glow Up »

**AFTER THINGS WITH** Martin ended the way that they did, Rae decided to swear men off for a while. She dove deeper into her studies and before she knew it, she was a senior.

The past couple of years had been bittersweet. True to her word, Whisper had educated and trained Rae until she had literally decreased her weight by half. The one-hundred-and-forty-pound beauty was damn near unrecognizable these days.

Whisper was the best at what she did, and Rae was confident that the outspoken girl would go far in the business.

Not only did Whisper ensure that Rae dropped the pounds, but she taught her how to do it in a healthy way to reduce her chances of having excess skin. Luckily for Rae since stretch marks were usually linked to genetics, she had never had any of those to worry about. Anyone who saw the brown skin beauty would never know that she'd nearly tipped the scales to three-hundred pounds at her heaviest.

Rae's training had started off a little rough in the beginning. No matter how hard she trained, the weight just wasn't coming off the way that Whisper thought that it should've been. Whisper was under the impression that Rae was closet eating and had nearly dropped her as a client until a positive HCG test revealed news that she could've gone without.

Rae was no fool, the morning following her humiliating night with Martin, she woke up and headed straight to the pharmacy and took the morning after pill. Apparently, that shit didn't work. Making the decision to terminate her pregnancy was a difficult one. She knew that she wasn't ready to have a child. It would've made completing school nearly impossible and she damn sure knew that she couldn't rely on Martin's crazy ass to help her out.

Approximately two months after she'd slept with him, Martin was finally able to post bail. He angrily blew her phone up cursing her out for not helping him out. She allowed him to entertain her for a while until she finally blocked him...but not before sending him the ultrasound picture of the fetus that she had already aborted. Now he would always wonder about the child that neither of them would ever have the pleasure of knowing.

Following the abortion, the weight melted away as expected. Rae soon realized that working out was a great stress reliever. After a couple of months, she started looking forward to exercising. Sometimes on Sundays she'd even workout on her own. Her body craved the physical activity and she learned that she couldn't even sleep without a good workout.

Her body was now beautifully sculpted and perhaps her most cherished attributes were her newly acquired abs and her juicy round ass. No amount of exercise would ever get her ass to budge.

Sadly, Whisper graduated a year before Rae, and she was gone just as quickly as she had arrived. Some people come into a person's life for a brief period of time and for a specific purpose. Rae believed that Whisper's purpose was to help her finally find her true self. Whisper had served her purpose and now she was gone. As Rae looked around her dorm room, the only remnants of Whisper ever having been there was Rae's snatched body.

Whisper had been offered a great job in South Carolina and didn't hesitate to accept it. She was more than happy to escape the blistering cold winters and overly sized rodents of New York.

Rae and Zo's senior year seemed to fly by faster than the previous years. Rae wanted to surprise her family and Afrika with her new body, so she had been avoiding them. Her family was heartbroken when she didn't even come home for the holidays.

She lied and told them that she was struggling with her classes and had to study in order to pass. While they found it strange because she always performed well, they gave her the benefit of the doubt. Why would she lie about not passing her classes?

During her senior year, Rae had done a lot of reflecting. She was homesick and no longer felt the need to run anymore. She applied and was accepted into three Dentistry Schools. She would break the exciting news to her family at her pre-dentistry graduation. They all assumed that she would continue her education in Missouri.

Rae had even convinced Zo that she couldn't bear to be

away from him, so he made the decision to return back home as well. He would hold his bachelor's degree in history and would be ready to enter the work force. She was so proud of her friend.

Rae knew that she still had another four years of school ahead of her. If she moved back to Texas, she knew that she already had a job waiting for her at her family's practice. She could work there as a dental assistant while she worked her way through school.

She was ready to buy a house and get settled too. She was done with living on campus and dealing with roommates. While Whisper had been a great roommate, the two heifers that followed weren't so great. She never even learned the second girl's name.

On graduation day, Rae and Zo waited patiently for their families and Afrika to arrive at the airport. She was so anxious to see how everyone would react to her transformation that she couldn't stop pacing about the floor.

"Best friend, please sit your happy ass down. You're starting to make me nervous." Zo said.

As she went to sit for the hundredth time, she spotted Ant and Sam headed in their direction. Rae took off towards her big brothers not even letting the six-inch heels slow her down. Once she reached them, she wrapped her arms around them both at the same time.

She squeezed them hard and for so long that she hadn't even realized when her parents and Afrika had joined in on the group hug.

After shedding some tears, her family and Afrika all begin to mention how great she looked and inquiring how she had shed so much weight. She was all smiles and had never felt more beautiful with all of the compliments tapping on her tympanic membranes. After relishing in her family's love, she looked over and saw that Zo was also being smothered with love from his own.

Over dinner that evening, Rae and Zo surprised their families by revealing that they would be returning home after their graduation ceremony the following day. Rae told them that she had decided to attend Texas A&M College of Dentistry in order to complete her studies. She also told them of her plans to purchase a house and start working for the family business in her free time.

Zo had accepted a teaching position at Bryan Adams High school. Teaching wasn't the most lucrative profession, but he sure as hell had job security. Zo promised his parents that after he grew accustomed to his schedule, that he would return to school for his master's degree.

Afrika had some great news of her own. While she had bypassed going to a traditional university, she had completed cosmetology school years prior and had paid her dues by slaving away in other people's shops. She was proud to announce that she was finally able to buy her own salon.

The trio were back together and stronger than ever. Things were surely looking up.

## « Chapter 14 If You Go Looking... »

**AFTER YEARS OF BEING** on her own, it felt so weird moving back home with her parents. Although Rae knew that it was temporary, she felt like a child again being back in her childhood bed. For some reason, her bed made her think of Prosper and how he was doing. How was married life treating him? Was he happy? Did he ever think of her at all?

After she had lurked and found out that he had gotten married years ago, she was never able to work up the nerve to snoop again. Like the old adage says, if you go looking for trouble, you'll surely find it.

The more she lay there thinking about him, the more she allowed her curiosity to get the best of her. Once she typed Prosper Collins into the search engine, it was too late to turn back.

"Damn it!" She groaned as she realized that he had finally made his social media accounts private.

Not one to accept defeat easily, a bright idea came to Rae. She smiled as she typed in Claryssa St. John.

"What the fuck?!" Rae huffed when no results were found.

"Oh, I'm so stupid!" The woman exclaimed popping herself on the forehead.

She then tried Claryssa Collins and a profile picture generated of Claryssa, Prosper and a little girl who appeared to be about two. Rae's heart shattered as she stared at the toddler who looked just like Prosper. Claryssa's account was private too, but it didn't matter because she didn't want to see anymore anyway.

"Well, I guess that answers that." Rae sulked to herself.

"I see your crazy ass still talks to yourself." Ant teased, catching the tail end of Rae's solo conversation.

"What the hell do you have on, sis? Don't think that because your ass is small now that I won't fuck you up about wearing that little skimpy shit Rae!" Her overprotective brother threatened as usual.

Rae just rolled her eyes, but didn't respond as she picked up her purse and followed him to his car. It was summertime in Texas. Ant should've been happy that she wasn't flouncing around in a thong bikini.

Both Ant and Sam had purchased beautiful houses within the last year and Rae wanted one for herself. Her brothers had turned the dope that they'd confiscated from her in high school into millions, so they thought it was only fair that they bought her a crib of her own. As far as they were concerned, she could have whatever house she wanted.

Ant was going to introduce his sister to his and Sam's real estate agent. He was young, but the little nigga had access to some of the dopest houses in the Dallas-Fort Worth area as well as its surrounding regions.

Ant smiled as he watched his little sister's face light up as they went from the modest houses that she had grew up in, to high end houses that she'd only seen on tv. They eventually pulled up to a house that was grander than Rae had ever seen in person.

She had butterflies as she anticipated seeing the inside. After her brother opened the car door for her and assisted her out, she trailed behind him up towards the house. There was already another very expensive white car parked in the driveway.

Before Ant could enter the code to the keypad, the heavy wooden door swung open. When the house's occupant stepped out into view, Rae's blood went cold. She damn near passed out because she had somehow managed to forget to breathe.

It couldn't be...what were the fucking odds??? She looked on as Ant and Prosper dapped each other up as if they had been acquainted their entire lives. For a moment the two appeared oblivious to her presence as they caught up on "man stuff".

Finally, Ant remembered and said, "Oh yeah Prosper, this is my baby sister Desirae who is looking for a house...Rae, this is my real estate agent Prosper. I know you'll make sure that she gets nothing but the best my dude. I wouldn't let no one else sell her a house."

Rae could feel Prosper looking at her with admiration. She could tell that he recognized her, but he was mostly in awe of her weight loss. She looked damn good and she knew it. Her natural curls had streaks of honey blonde in them. The red shorts that she wore barely contained her meaty ass cheeks and her mid-drift white tube top boldly showcased her hard-earned abs.

Grinning, she decided to play with him. She extended her manicured hand to Prosper and said, "Hello, Prosper is it? I am very pleased to meet you."

Ant had to nudge Prosper from his trance before he was able to return the gesture. Ant just shook his head at the young guy. He knew that he was married, so he wasn't too worried about his obvious attraction to his sister.

Rae was raised better than to get involved with a married man, but just to be on the safe side he asked, "So how are Claryssa and little Bobbie doing?"

He internally smiled as he watched as Rae's body stiffened and her hand recoiled from Prosper's touch.

Prosper felt some type away about the way that Ant fronted him out, however, it was short lived. After all he was indeed married, and Ant's massive checks always cleared.

Getting back into business mode Prosper said, "It's nice to meet you too, Desirae. There's actually been a slight change in plans. I just found out that this house was just taken off the market, plus I think this muthafucka is haunted or some shit anyway.

Don't fret, I have others to show you. This is how this works; I will show you three houses all within very different price ranges and you will let me know which one you like from there. We will start off low and then go high.

The catch is, you have to see all three before you decide."

"Well, what if I don't like any of the three that you show me?" Rae inquired.

Both Prosper and Ant smiled knowingly. He then replied, "If that happens, then that will be a first, but we will cross that bridge when we get there Ms. Desirae."

Rae and Ant followed behind Prosper as he led the two of them to two beautiful houses. She personally would've settled for the first one, however, she had to see all three before she made her decision. Once reaching the third house, she knew immediately that it was way out of her price range.

The two-story house came equipped with five bedrooms, four bathrooms, a study, a home theater in the basement, a pool in the backyard and a five-car garage. The landscaping was just beautiful. She almost didn't go in because she just knew that it was too much. Why'd she need such a big house when it was just her?

Reluctantly she got out and entered the massive door. Upon seeing the open spaced foyer, she immediately envisioned all of the parties that she could host there. The spacious kitchen was certainly constructed for some good southern cooking. The stainless-steel appliances alone had to be more than some made in a year.

After spending over an hour touching, drooling and inspecting everything, Ant whispered to Prosper that he believed that a decision had been made. He made Prosper promise not to disclose the full six-hundred-thousand-dollar price tag to his sister until closing. Then he wouldn't be able to hide what would be printed on the contracts.

"Just tell her that the house is half of what I'm paying for it. Tell her that the previous owners are just extremely motivated to sale or some shit. Hell, figure out something." Ant ordered.

"Word, I got you bro." Prosper assured with a cheesy smile on his face.

Do I need

## « Chapter 15 Sistahood »

THE DAY THAT RAE closed on her house was one of the happiest moments of her life. She cursed Ant out for lying about how much the house had cost, yet when he told her that he could see if Propser still had the cheaper houses available she damn near killed him. She was already attached to her house by the time her closing date arrived. She already had her house furnished...at least mentally.

With very little coaxing, she got Zo to agree to move in with her so that she wouldn't be completely alone.

She always felt safer with Zo around. He was after all her oldest friend and had always protected her when her brothers weren't around. Zo was sick of living with his parents and was in the process of looking for an apartment when she asked.

His parents were great, but he was not used to living with them anymore. Afrika was extended the invitation too, but she was seeing someone and was in the process of moving in with her new boo. Home girl was doing the damn thing!

For the next couple of months, Rae and Zo worked diligently to make their house a home. Since there was no mortgage to pay, the pair just split the cost of the utilities and cable. When August came around, Rae started Dentistry school while Zo started his career as a history teacher. Practically being raised in a dental office by two dentists as parents made dentistry school easy for Rae.

She still had to study and take her education seriously, but she was much less stressed than many of her classmates. She had already received hands on experience from the best in the game. By the time Thanksgiving rolled around, the house was looking great enough for Rae and Zo to host Thanksgiving at their house that year. Of course, it somewhat doubled as a housewarming party since they'd never officially had one.

Rae, Zo, Afrika, Valentina, and Afrika's mom, Lonnie were enlisted to do all of the cooking...of course. Zo's mom, Tinisha meant well, however the beautiful woman couldn't boil water. Instead, she was tasked with decorating and shopping for what was needed. It all worked out perfectly.

The men...well their contribution was to keep their credit cards on standby.

"Damn, it's smelling good as hell up in here! How much longer before we can eat?!" Sam's hungry ass impatiently inquired.

Instead of waiting for an answer, he went to lift up the lid that housed the cabbage. Before he could even get a peek, let alone a taste, Valentina popped him in the back of his head while proceeding to fuss at him in Spanish. That's how he knew she was aggravated. The hungry young man was a lot like his sister and never gave up easily. He stubbornly snatched up two of the homemade dinner rolls that were cooling off and dashed into a nearby bedroom, locking the door behind himself before a screaming Valentina could catch him.

"Tu pequeña mierda!!!" The flustered woman yelled to her youngest son as he busied himself with his stolen treats on the other side of the door.

"Who's a little shit?" Valentina's confused husband, James asked as he returned with several cases of beer for the guys.

"No one, sweetheart." The spicy Dominican replied as she began to make out with her sexy husband.

"Ewwww...haven't you guys made out enough over the years?!" Rae asked in disgust.

"Tomen apuntes, hija. If you're lucky, you'll know what it's like to experience a love like this one day." Valentina stated genuinely hoping that her youngest child would be as blessed in the love department as she had been.

Although she always got on her parents for their never-ending PDA, the truth was that she loved watching how much they still adored and enjoyed one another after so many years of marriage.

As the men, excluding Ant as he was away on a business trip, busied themselves with the game, the ladies and Zo put the final touches on their Thanksgiving feast. Rae decided that she couldn't ignore her full bladder anymore and asked her best friend to keep a watchful eye on her turkey and pot roast.

Before she made it to her master bedroom, she stopped once she reached the spare bedroom that separated her and Zo.

Listening at the door she could certainly hear voices, but couldn't decipher whose voices it was.

She discreetly turned the doorknob and discovered that it had been locked. Now her curiosity heightened. It was her house and there was no privacy in her shit as far as she was concern with the exception of Zo. She reached into her pocket and retrieved the skeleton key. She smiled when it quietly unlocked the door permitting her access.

Twisting the knob, she quickly pushed the heavy door open. Rae screamed loudly when she walked in on Afrika riding Sam as if her life depended on it. She hadn't intentionally screamed the way that she had and immediately regretted it when the rest of the guests in the house came to investigate. While Sam looked unbothered, a mortified Afrika hid under the covers and profusely apologized to both Sam's parents and her mom.

After a little teasing, everyone soon returned to the game and the kitchen. It took Sam and Lonnie over an hour to talk Afrika into leaving the bedroom. She was quiet for the remainder of the evening. Rae felt so terrible that she didn't even bother asking her friend about the incident. However, that didn't stop Zo's nosy ass from inquiring.

Afrika and Sam had apparently been seeing each other for years. She never wanted to tell Rae because she didn't want it to affect their friendship. It was Sam who had purchased her beauty salon for her, and he was the mysterious *boo* who she was living with.

It was funny because Afrika was so convinced that Rae wouldn't want to be her friend any longer, yet Rae now felt as if she had truly gained a sister. Sam never really brought any girls around, so she knew that her brother must've been serious about her.

Ant on the other hand was a hoe. That negro always had a different chick on his arms. He would probably never settle down with just one woman. Being a dentist, he had too many women throwing themselves at him to just settle down with one. The apple certainly didn't fall far...

Just as everyone was about to sit down and eat, in walked Prosper along with Claryssa and their daughter. That was rapidly becoming one of the most eventful Thanksgivings ever.

## « Chapter 16 Welcome To The Neighborhood »

"HEY SIS, I HOPE THAT you don't mind that I invited Prosper and his family. He told me that they weren't cooking this year and with them living nearby, I figured, why not?" Sam naively asked.

She couldn't believe that her brother had nonchalantly invited the man that she'd been in love with for years over to her house along with his family! She was supposed to be his family.

Standing up, Rae walked over to Prosper and his family and took the food that they were carrying.

Prosper stated, "Here you go, Rae. I normally get my clients a bottle of wine, but I've been so busy that I forgot to send it. Well, I hope you like it." He offered.

Claryssa said, "I have always loved this house, but my husband would never buy it for me. I guess for now I'll continue admiring it from our yard," while handing Rae the Patti pies that she picked up earlier that day. The sorry bitch couldn't even bring over homemade pies.

"Oh, from your yard? How far do you guys live from here?" Rae inquired almost scared to ask.

"Girl, not far at all! We live right next door! Welcome to the neighborhood!" Claryssa cheesed.

The heifer had a nerve not to even remember Rae and that annoyed her too. Why in the hell would Prosper sell her a house right next door to him and his family? She'd planned on living in her house for forever, but surely, she couldn't bear to look at the two of them all in love for the rest of her life, could she?

Sizing up Claryssa, she determined that she still looked good. Her stomach protruded outwards more than she remembered, but aside from that, she still had it going on.

"Damn P, I didn't know that you lived next door man." Sam replied while internally questioning Prosper's motives for moving his sister in next door. He was wondering what type of fuck shit he had in mind.

"I didn't think it would be a big deal. It's a house that I would've moved my own sister into. I figured I could look out for her and besides is it not a great house?" Prosper asked looking hurt.

"The house is great. Thanks for coming guys. Who is this

little cutie?" Rae gushed looking at the pretty little girl who was a perfect mixture of both of her parents.

"This is Bobbie, but we just call her BJ. Say hello BJ!" Claryssa cooed speaking to the girl as if she was much younger.

"Hel-lo." BJ said shyly while hiding behind her father.

"Well, have a seat niggas and let's dig in!" A hungry Sam declared already chewing on a piece of ham that he'd swiped from the table.

## « Chapter 17 Sexually Catfished »

"**Soooooo heifer**! Spill it!" Rae demanded as Afrika braided her natural hair into lemonade braids.

Hell, she had patiently waited for the specifics on how her and Sam hooked up for long enough. She knew that it was still a sensitive subject since she had literally caught them both in the act, but Rae decided that she was going to get over it that day.

"Truthfully, I had always found him attractive, but assumed that he only saw me as his little sister's annoying friend...and I wasn't wrong. He didn't start pursuing me until one day I received a direct message from him on Facebook. I suppose he liked the pictures that I had posted that day because he was on some 'you sure have grown up' type of shit.

I thought it was cute and I liked the attention. He was always so respectful and attuned to my feelings. You know that

I didn't really have experience dealing with men outside of Zo and well you know... Anyway, at some point he stopped being the big brother that used to squirt whipped cream on our faces in our sleep. Somewhere along the way he transitioned into a sexy man. I love your brother and I know that he loves me too." Afrika affirmed with a smile.

"But I thought that you were going to wait until after you were married to have sex?" Rae asked.

"You know when we are young, we map out our entire lives and the way they should be no matter how unrealistic our visions may be. It isn't that abstaining from sex was unrealistic, I was just ready. I didn't want to wait. He's the one...the only guy for me, so I didn't feel the need to hold out on something we both wanted." Afrika admitted.

"Ya little freak!" Rae teased.

"You've been holding out on us hoe! We need details! Did you like it?" Zo asked.

"Not too many details though, I'm not trying to hear about my brother's little ding-a-ling!" Rae stated with a sour look on her face.

Afrika smacked her red painted lips and said, "Wrong already heifer, my baby's *DICK* is huge and curved just right that it hits my..."

"Aht aht aht bitch! Less details. Now proceed again." Rae belted in disgust.

"As I was saying, it hurt like hell the first time and it sometimes hurts now, but like Zo said in high school, it hurts in a good way now. I think the fact that I love the fuck out of Sam makes our love making that much better. I've never been with anyone else sexually and I honestly can't imagine sexing someone who I wasn't in love with. How do prostitutes and strippers give up such intimacy to perfect strangers?" Afrika asked genuinely puzzled.

"I don't know friend. Maybe those Ben Franks have a way of making them love those tricks for a short amount of time." Zo answered.

"Enough about me! Desirae, what happened on your date with Mr. Legend?" Afrika stated and stared hoping to take the attention off of herself.

Taking a deep breath, Rae exhaled the entire story of how her recent date with Legend went.

*"You know Legend had been eyeballing me since the very first day our program started, but I ignored him and kept it professional. You know they say to never shit where you eat so I always took some Imodium before class...if you know what I mean.*

*Anyway, he and I just happened to get paired up together in class, so I had no choice, but to communicate with his ass. Don't get me wrong, he is chocolate and cute, but the issue is, he knows it too. He's conceited and arrogant and to be perfectly honest it turned me off. He is one of those people who always thinks they're right, even when they aren't.*

*Doing the project with him was a thorn in my ass. He completely took over the entire assignment and only his ideas were good ones. Finally, I cussed his ass out and told him to do this damn thing by himself...which his cocky ass did, and we got an A while all of the other groups got B's and C's.*

*I had to give it to him, he did great on the assignment. Had we done what I suggested, we wouldn't have received an A. As a peace offering for being a bitch to him, I offered to treat Legend to dinner. It was platonic of course, at least on my end.*

We were actually having a good time surprisingly. He was still arrogant, however, his great sense of humor was able to shine through.

Through our conversation I realized that where he came from, he had to be cocky and confident. He is the first person in his family to attend college, let alone become a dentist. As we are stuffing our faces, in walks Prosper and Claryssa. I tried to act as though I didn't see their asses, but Prosper's eyes seemed as though they were magnetically drawn to me.

Shortly after he and Claryssa were seated, she got up to go to the bathroom so Prosper used that opportunity to crash my platonic date.

He walked over mean mugging Legend. When he reached our table, I didn't say anything to him, which really made things awkward. After all, I wasn't concerned about his feelings when he had a whole wife in the restroom.

Legend took the lead by asking, "Hey brother, are you lost? Can we help you with something?"

I smiled knowing that I wasn't in the presence of a sucker. Legend could hold his own.

Rage took over Prosper's handsome face, but he only stated, "Nah bruh. I thought I saw someone I knew."

With that he turned to go back to his table as Claryssa was coming out of the bathroom. He glared at me until we left. Legend asked about Prosper several times throughout the night. I admitted that I knew him but didn't feel it necessary to discuss him any further.

Legend had a three-year-old daughter with his ex-fiancée Monika. He claimed that her poor spending habits and shopping addiction drew them apart. He reported that at one point she had been the love of his life, but time and circumstances had changed that. He claimed to really like me and told me that he wanted to get to know me better.

Over the course of a month, we virtually spent all of our free time together. I even met his daughter Portia aka Tia a few times. Monika wasn't thrilled about that, but he assured me that he didn't give a damn. Tia was a sweet child and quickly became attached to me.

Things were going great and I was letting my guard down with him. Hell, I was even thinking about Prosper a little less.

One evening Legend sent me a picture of his dick. Guys I can't even lie, it was so big, juicy and pretty that my pearl was throbbing. He soon called and asked if I liked what I saw. The phone gave me the courage that I ordinarily wouldn't have had face to face.

He was clearly drunk and talking super freaky. I was horny and curious, so I allowed my pussy to lead me to his front porch. I was sober, but I was drunken by lust. I wanted him to make me feel good.

I wanted the ecstasy that the love songs talk about. I wanted the lyrics to caress me. I entered his house looking and smelling good. All I had on was a thin form fitting jacket and nothing else.

I was ready for Legend to reenact all of the nasty things that he promised to do to me.

Legend led me to his room and quickly removed my jacket from around me. At first, I self-consciously hesitated, but then I remembered who the fuck I was. Confidently, I began to suck imaginary milk from my breasts. I must have been doing a great job, because he couldn't take his eyes off of me. I softly instructed him to remove his clothes too and he happily obliged.

His shirt was the first to go and I was very impressed by his chiseled upper body. His cocky ass knew it too because he seemed to flex extra hard with a sexy smirk on his face. When it got time to remove his pants, he seemed to shy away and turn away from me as he removed and kicked them away.

I was deprived of seeing the first dick that entered me so I damn sure wasn't going to be blind fucked again.

"Turn around and let me see it." Rae asked shyly.

"Ummm, alright but it's still not all the way hard so it looks a little small right now." He stated remorsefully.

"Boy please there is nothing small..." Rae voice trailed off.

"Nooo bitch! Don't say it! Please, don't say it!" Zo squealed.

"Fuck him, whisper it to me bitch. I need to know! What happened next!" Afrika exclaimed as she stopped braiding for a moment.

"Why did his ass have a three, maybe four-inch dick y'all?! I don't know whose dick he sent me...but that shit was not his...which is even more disturbing!!! What guy texts a female a picture of another guy's dick?! Did he not think that I'd notice that half of his dick was missing?!" Rae hissed growing heated all over again.

Both of her friends' jaws dropped in shock.

Rae then continued, "You know, it's not like I'm a size whore or anything, I just didn't appreciate being "dick-fished", ya know?"

"Yeah, yeah, yeah...fuck all that! Did you still let him make that cat drool?" Zo's vulgar ass asked.

"First of all, ewwww Zo. Why do you have to be extra? Why can't you just ask if we had sex the normal way?"

"Heifer, when have I ever been normal? I'll wait..." Zo glanced down at his new Rolex dramatically.

"Anyway, what happened next, Rae?" Afrika asked rolling her eyes at Zo.

"What else could I do? We had sex. I couldn't have just left his little Peter just standing up looking at me. I didn't even bring the shit up to him. I just pretended as if that bite size pickle was normal. It was terrible.

He went down on me and it was just a mess. I'm not an expert, but I don't think teeth are needed for cunnilingus. His stroke was weak and luckily for me he lasted less than two minutes. He wanted to cuddle, so I laid in a wet spot all night wondering what I was doing with my life.

I'm done with these fools. Sex is so overrated. I was sexually catfished. Is that even a thing?!

## « Chapter 18 Know Your Worth »

"**WHAT IS GOING ON WITH** you Prosper?" Claryssa inquired with an attitude.

Typically, her husband was always in the mood to make her cheeks clap however after fifteen minutes of giving him head, his dick was limper than a spaghetti noodle.

Pushing her head out of his lap, Prosper stated, "Nothing, I just got a lot on my mind C. Work shit mostly."

"But work is going great though, baby. This has by far been our most profitable year." Claryssa rebutted.

"It isn't always about the money, as a matter of fact, I really don't want to talk about it right now. It's been a long day and we both have to get up early in the morning to get you to the airport on time." Prosper said.

"You're absolutely right. I'm sorry for pressuring you babe." Claryssa said woefully.

Prosper hated arguing with his wife. Especially since he knew the true source behind his flaccid member.

Strange feelings had been resurfacing for the doll faced woman next door and it was becoming harder to keep them at bay. It was funny how he had literally gone years without seeing her, yet now she was all he could think about since she moved back in town.

Prosper knew that moving Rae into the house next door was brazen and foolish, but when he laid eyes on her for the first time after all those years, all of his senses went out the window.

Desirae had always been one of the most beautiful women to Prosper, even being morbidly obese, however she was now a certified knockout from head to toe. One of his biggest regrets was letting her slip through his fingers.

He wasn't blind, he knew that she had a crush on him, but he couldn't be with her the way she deserved due to her size. He didn't want to have to fuck anyone up for coming at her sideways. Back then it was just easier to ignore what was staring him in the face in order to keep the peace.

By the time that he had gotten to the point that he didn't care about what other's thought, it was too late. Rae didn't want anything to do with him based on what she had found inside of his bag years ago. He tried to explain the truth many times over, yet it all fell on deaf ears. Once she had moved away to Missouri, he finally accepted defeat and threw in the towel.

Prosper honestly never expected to see the brown

beauty again, but there she stood on that fateful day. Prosper had met Ant and Sam a year and a half prior while he was getting his teeth cleaned. He overheard the two of them conversing about purchasing houses and didn't hesitate to give them his business cards. He could tell that the men had money...more money than the average dentist typically had so he happily showed them both upscale houses that he knew they'd love.

Fast forward eighteen months later, Prosper didn't think much of it when Ant approached him about finding a home for his sister. Prosper had a knack for reading people and knew almost immediately what his clients were looking for.

As soon as he laid eyes on the "new" Desirae in her form fitting shorts, he knew that there would only be one house that he would be selling her. What Ant didn't know was that Prosper would've paid half of the cost of the house in order to persuade her to move into that house. Luckily for his bank account, he didn't have to resort to that.

The months following Rae moving in, he had tried his hardest to stay away. Despite those efforts, he still found himself sitting outside more hoping to catch brief glimpses of her. As crazy as it was, he had pretty much familiarized himself with her hectic schedule.

His new fixation on the woman next door was now affecting his intimacy with his spouse. He and Claryssa had always been good in that department. To be honest, oftentimes that seemed to be all they had aside from BJ.

Seeing Rae at the restaurant with that man, nearly made Prosper act a damn fool. The only thing that stopped him was the realization that he had no right. He was married and Rae was virtually a stranger. Who was he to show his natural ass on her date?

It just wasn't his place...at least not then. Since seeing that clown with Rae, Prosper noticed him coming and going from her house. Prosper was no homo and concluded that while the guy was okay, he didn't have shit on him. His pockets damn sure wasn't fatter.

One evening while shoveling the snow in front of his house, a noise drew his attention over to Rae's yard.

Glancing over, he noticed that peanut head dude making his way out to his car. After waiting for the windshield to defrost, he took off without adequately getting the snow off from the top and rear of his car.

"Lazy ass nigga," Prosper mumbled.

Once he finished his yard, he walked over to Rae's yard and proceeded to get her driveway together. He assumed that she must have been watching, because as soon as he was finished, her front door opened.

His eyes doubled in size when they focused in on her sexy frame posing seductively in the doorway. She had on a white short silk robe that barely reached her toned thighs. He was so preoccupied with molesting her with his eyes that he hadn't noticed that she was talking to him.

"Hello! Hello! Earth to Prosper!" Rae called out with a bright Colgate smile.

"Hunh, did you say something?" Prosper asked.

"Uhhh, I've said plenty. I was thanking you for getting my driveway, stairs and walkway together for me. You know you really didn't have to do that. My dad told me that he was going to come out and do it tomorrow morning before work." Rae claimed.

"It was nothing. I don't mind. I had to do my own yard,

so, I figured I'd just come over and get you together before I retired for the evening. I'll bill you for my services later." He joked.

She laughed showcasing her sexy dimples before saying, "Here, I made you some hot chocolate. I saw you out here working hard, so I figured this might help warm you back up a little."

Proper glanced over towards his house and wondered if he should. Claryssa and BJ were fast asleep when he had left the house. A cup of hot chocolate wouldn't hurt would it?

Sensing his uncertainty, Rae hammered the final nail in the coffin when she stated, "I put extra marshmallows in it, and I have the fireplace going..."

Rae was so sexy and smelled so good as he approached her that not even the freezing February temperature could keep his woody at bay. It's funny because he couldn't get and maintain an erection these days even being inside of his wife's warm mouth.

After he closed the door behind him, she handed him the warm cup of hot chocolate. She then led him to a set of cozy chairs placed directly in front of the fireplace as promised. Rae was sipping on what appeared to be wine.

Her pretty curls were messily arranged on top of her head, yet she was still gorgeous. When she sat down in front of him, she crossed her juicy legs and Prosper could see that she wasn't wearing anything under the short robe. His dick jumped when he noticed her smooth bare kitty smiling at him.

Rae smiled inwardly too, because she knew what she was doing. She had been dating Legend since their first sexual encounter and things hadn't improved at all. He was a good guy and she really enjoyed spending time with him, however she dreaded the sexual component of their relationship.

She was always finding creative ways to get out of doing it, but she had to be careful because last month she had used the "I'm on my period" excuse too many times. Today she pretended to not feel well and she had told Legend that she had diarrhea. What better way to kill a libido than a sudden case of the shits?

When Rae saw Prosper outside in her yard, she felt a little embarrassed because she knew that he had most likely seen Legend leave and that he hadn't even bothered to pave a safe path for her to get out of her driveway. However, she didn't allow the shame to stop her from jumping in the shower and throwing on her expensive perfume.

Noticing his snow-covered boots, she stood up and kneeled in front of him. Untying the laces, she removed them along with his socks from his feet. She walked into the closest bathroom and grabbed some massage oils. When she returned, she scooted her chair closer to Prosper and placed both of his feet on top of her lap. She was relieved when she noted his feet to be well cared for.

"Oh, they're soft too." She said flirtatiously.

She truly didn't expect him to allow her to touch him in such a manner, but his eyes literally closed as she went to work on his feet. While most people despised feet, they didn't bother her. After all she had chosen a profession in which she'd be dedicating her time working in rotten mouths. She massaged Zo's big size fourteens all the time and vice versa.

Prosper had gotten so into the massage that he allowed fragmented moans to escape from his plump lips. She also noticed the huge tent that had formed in his pants. She wanted to touch it. She wanted to see what it felt like in her hands, so she methodically traded his feet for his anaconda.

His eyes snapped open when he felt her small hand caress his manhood. He could see the desire and curiosity in her eyes. He knew what he was doing was wrong, but as he locked eyes with Rae, he felt himself powerlessly lift up his hips and slide his pants down to his ankles before kicking them off.

Her breathing became haggard as she again took a hold of his dick and began to play with it as if it were a valuable toy. She stroked and massaged it and became excited when precum oozed from its thick tip.

He knew that his ten-inch Hershey bar was probably bigger than anything else she'd experienced and as bad as he wanted to fuck her, he knew that he couldn't. He vaguely remembered that he was married, and the promise that he made to stay true to her years ago.

As Rae continued to stroke him with her left hand, she began to rub on her drooling center with the other one. The sight was just too much because he soon found himself on his knees kneeling before her. As soon as his tongue flicked against her clit, her thick thighs tightly coiled around his head.

If she constricted any harder, he was convinced that his facial features would forever be embedded into her juicy center. Within seconds of licking, sucking, humming and slurping up her pussy, Rae convulsed and cried out as her very first orgasm rippled through her stomach. Tears literally spilled from her eyes once she reopened them.

Even though her pearl was extremely sensitive, Prosper didn't stop his tongue's attack. Over the next thirty minutes the orgasm giver, donated four more nuts until Rae begged for mercy.

"Fuck me, Prosper! Fuck me!!!" Desirae demanded breathlessly. Her face was saturated with tears of ecstasy, yet she had never looked more beautiful.

That's all Prosper needed to hear as he swiftly placed himself at her entrance. Grabbing his thick penis, he rubbed it up and down her slit coating himself with her juices. He bore into her eyes and nearly lost it when she sexily bit down on her bottom lip.

Her eyes were low and filled with pure lust. She drew in a sharp breath as the pressure from being penetrated reached her brain. She had never felt so utterly full in her life. Prosper was stretching her out and it did hurt, but the suckling of her breasts made the pain below vanish.

When he reached her bottom, they both sighed loudly. With closed eyes, the pair remained motionless as they relished in the pleasure that their connection was emitting. It was then that she decided that she loved that man. As Prosper attempted to plunge into her ocean again, the familiar ringtone reserved especially for his wife began to blare from inside of his coat pocket.

Deciding to plunge his thick dick back inside of Rae one more time, he closed his eyes in ecstasy and rested his cheek against hers. He knew that he had her full attention.

"Desirae, always know your worth. Never mess with a nigga who ignores a driveway full of snow. Never fuck with a nigga who ignores a full trash can. Never fuck with a nigga who obviously isn't satisfying you sexually and lastly, never mess with a married nigga. You deserve better than what I can give you. We can't let this happen again." Prosper told a devastated Desirae.

When he withdrew from her body, she felt an immediate sense of loss and wanted to cry, but she didn't.

She remained motionless as she watched Prosper get redressed and retreat back towards his house.

## « Chapter 19 Megan Thee Stallion »

"MAN CUZZO! THIS SHIT is so fire!!!" Prosper complimented as he greedily scarfed down the fried ribs that Charlie had been experimenting with.

Charlie always used Prosper as his guinea pig and Prosper didn't mind being used at all.

"Well BJ and Serena, what do you little muthafuckas think?" Charlie asked his little cousins who were also there to weigh in on whether or not the fried ribs should be added to the menu.

Prosper just shook his head at his crazy ass cousin's poor choice of words as he resumed smashing his ribs.

Serena shouted, "Charlie these are the best ribs ever!"

While BJ simply gave Charlie two thumbs up.

"I guess it's been decided. Fried ribs it is. I appreciate you fam." Charlie stated sincerely to the hungry trio.

Charlie was always looking into expanding his menu and thanks to his open mind, no one else offered a more diverse menu in town. Prosper, his sister and his daughter ate at the restaurant more than they ate at home. Claryssa's idea of dinner was a big bucket of KFC with sides. Prosper didn't even like KFC.

"Hey Charlie, let me holla at you really quick." Prosper said to his cousin after cleaning his plate.

Charlie nodded and followed Prosper to a table just a couple of tables away from the children. Cautiously looking around Prosper whispered, "Hey man, I fucked up. And I fucked up bad."

Charlie was now on high alert because he rarely saw anything razzle his cousin and, in that moment, Prosper looked distraught.

"Yo, what's up man? You know I saved some of those bangers, right? Do I need to pay someone a visit? You know I ride for you, right?" Charlie stated genuinely.

"Naw, it's nothing like that, but somewhat related to those bangers. Remember the shorty, Desirae who helped me out the night we robbed that fool on Peevly drive? Well, she moved back here from Missouri and nigga, why did my stupid ass move her right next door to me?" Prosper admitted shaking his head.

He knew that it was a dumb idea, however saying it out loud confirmed that his decision was even dumber than he'd previously thought.

"You did what?! Fool, what would possess your jughead ass to do some fuck shit like that? Claryssa is going to beat both of yalls asses." Charlie announced bewildered by his little cousin's admission.

Typically, he was the one who made the stupid mistakes, not Prosper.

"I know. I know man. It's crazy because it was her brothers, Ant and Sam who took the work from our robbery and now, I see how those niggas are so laced with cash. But that's not it. So, check it, she used to be fat as hell my nigga. Like Rasputia big...dude, why is she built like Megan Thee Stallion now. She is so dope man!

I tried to keep my distance from her chocolate ass, the Lord knows that I have, but one night I slipped up...well sort of. I kind of fucked her, but not really you know. I didn't nut or nothing like that. Does that shit count?" Prosper inquired truly wanting to know.

Charlie's goofy ass fell out laughing.

"P, how do you 'kind of' fuck a bitch?! Either you stuck your dick in her or you didn't. I don't care what no one says, even if I slide up in a broad once and she changes her mind, I've officially fucked so it doesn't matter. Let me ask you this, if I go over to your house and just dick stroke Claryssa once, would you consider that fucking or 'kind of' fucking?" Charlie schooled his cousin.

After watching a scowl form on Prosper's face, Charlie knew that he had made his point, perhaps a little too well.

"Judging by the angry look on your face, I'd say you know damn well that the shitty logic that you've concocted to make yourself feel better about the situation is just that...shitty logic. Nigga wipe that frown up off your face, you know I can't do shit with your non-cooking ass wife. Plus, she's too damn bony for me, however I'll be more than happy to take Meg Thee Stallion up off your hands since you really didn't fuck her *for real.*" Charlie teased.

"Charlie, you can't have my Claryssa or my "Megan", especially since I can't have her. She is seeing this lame who is definitely going to know that I've been up in that pussy the next time he hits it. I stretched that shit the fuck out in two strokes!" Prosper exclaimed knowingly.

"So, what are you going to do about your situation?" Charlie asked.

"What can I do? You know my situation with Claryssa man. I have feelings for her, and we have BJ together. She's been there for a nigga. I owe her." Prosper sighed.

"Look man, I said this before and I'll say it again, do what your heart is telling you to do. You don't owe Claryssa shit. Although you won't admit it out loud or to yourself, I know that you don't love her. At least not in the capacity that a husband should love his wife. I'm your cousin and will always back you up no matter what...right or wrong. If "Ms. Megan" makes you happy, then I'm here for the shit."

The cousins dapped up and promised to meet up later to shoot some pool. What they didn't realize was that someone was listening and had heard the entire exchange between the two men.

## « Chapter 20 Blast From The Past »

**"I THOUGHT I TOLD HER** ass to stop fucking with that sorry ass dude." Prosper whispered to himself as he noticed that Rae's little boyfriend had just pulled up to the front of her house.

"What was that, bae?" Claryssa asked forcing her attention away from the rachet reality tv show that she claimed that she could never miss.

"Nothing C. Absolutely nothing." Prosper mumbled miserably.

Since his encounter with Rae, he had grown to resent Claryssa and all of her shortcomings. He was convinced that he had wifed up the wrong woman, but what could he do about it now. He had made his bed and now he was dealing with it.

Pausing her beloved tv show, Claryssa walked over to her husband and unfastened his zipper as she got on her knees. To both of their surprise, he was hard as a brick.

"Ssssssssss!" Prosper hissed when he entered her voluptuous lips.

Claryssa had always given official head. Grabbing a fistful of the synthetic hair that he'd paid for; he began to thrust in and out of his wife's warm mouth...only it wasn't his wife that he was fantasizing about. In his mind he was making love to Rae's velvety mouth and it felt incredible. After nearly causing Claryssa to choke, he bent her over and swiftly entered her from behind.

"Ohhhh Prosper! Mmmhhmmmm daddy! Just like that!" She screamed as she threw her fat ass back at him.

In response, he loudly slapped both of her ass cheeks as he continued to play peekaboo with her pink elastic band. It had been some time since he'd been inside of some pussy, so he felt his nut quickly approaching. Never being a selfish lover, he began to deep stroke Claryssa upwards.

He could tell by the alterations in her breathing and trembling of her body that she was close to the edge. He finished her off by slipping a moist finger into her tight asshole. Claryssa started hitting opera worthy notes as she sprayed her husband with sex juice.

Before allowing Claryssa to come down from her orgasmic high, Prosper's strokes hastened as he prepared for takeoff. Just as he reached the point of no returned, he snatched his meat out of his wife and released his seeds into the palm of his hand. Claryssa hated when he unloaded on her. After catching his breath, he walked to the bathroom to get cleaned up so that he could meet up with his cousin.

"Dang son! This shit is too clean!" Charlie admired looking at Prosper's midnight blue convertible Mercedes C-Class.

"Oh, I got this a couple of weeks ago. I got a good deal on it too if you're interested." Prosper offered.

"For sure, hook it up." Charlie declared while excitedly rubbing his hands together.

The two blasted Nipsey Hussle and bobbed their heads as they made the twenty-five-minute commute to their favorite pool hall. Once they arrived, Prosper handed Reese a well-known crackhead forty dollars to keep an eye out on his new ride. Reese was loyal, well as loyal as a crackhead could be.

Prosper knew that Reese would guard his car with his life. Mack's Pool Hall wasn't in the greatest area, but it was always full of laughs and surprises. The two cousins took turns whooping each other's asses on the pool table, darts and in the arcade room in the back. When Claryssa began to blow Prosper's phone up, he knew that was his cue to take his black ass home.

"Damn man, she is always calling just as the fun is getting started! Megan is starting to look better and better every day." Charlie huffed.

Prosper laughed and said, "Her name isn't Megan nigga, it's Desirae."

"Megan...Desirae...same shit!" Charlie's drunk ass slurred.

"Man bring your drunk ass on!" Prosper playfully yelled at his crazy ass cousin.

As the men exited the pool hall, Prosper smiled when he saw that Reese was still standing guard next to his car. His smile soon faded when he noticed how nervous Reese looked. His eyes almost appeared apologetic, but his mouth remained stationary. Assuming that someone had hit his car or some shit, Prosper power walked towards his car leaving an inebriated Charlie stumbling behind him.

As Prosper reached Reese to ask why he was looking so stressed, the older man began to apologize over and over again. Before Prosper could figure out why he was so sorry, gunshots began to loudly sound off. It seemed as if they were coming from all different directions. Prosper was shook as he noticed a large hole form in between Reese's eyes before his body dropped to the pavement with a loud thud.

In shock Prosper stared at the blood flowing from the man's cranium. The loud pops were no longer audible as his inner ears was no longer able to transport sounds. A piercing pain to his right lower abdomen snapped him out of his stupor.

"Ahhhhhh shit!" Prosper yelled through clenched teeth.

Suddenly he remembered Charlie and he took off towards his cousin. Without thinking he stumbled into the line of fire and was quickly hit by two more bullets. Despite trying to continue walking, the excruciating pain in his left leg made him drop quicker than a whore's panties.

Prosper resorted to Army crawling. He just had to make sure that his cousin was okay. Every time he moved, he thought that he would pass out from the agonizing pain. He couldn't even see straight due to the blinding pain.

At some point he had managed to crawl into a motionless body. He knew that it could only be one person.

The gunmen assuming that they'd adequately silenced their targets had already retreated before the police came.

"Fuck Charlie! Man, what the fuck! Please be okay. I can't tell your mama that you're gone man. Please be okay!" Prosper chanted over and over until darkness consumed him.

## « Chapter 21 A Huge Favor »

"**AWWW DON'T BE A** sore loser!" Rae chuckled as she watched Legend pout.

She had pulled out her throwback Super Nintendo and had once again crushed him in Super Mario Bros. 3.

"Pay up!" She demanded with her hand out.

Feigning disappointment, he gave Rae the last of the banana flavored Laffy Taffy candies. Rae absolutely loved them, but knew that they didn't love her. Legend would get her five of them every Friday and then he'd try to eat them all. Rae knew that she'd beat him, so she had no issue with wagering with her beloved candy.

"Awww, I'll split it with you." She laughed as she bit off the larger piece.

Legend happily accepted the other piece from her banana coated mouth. This led to a full on make out session. Soon Legend was on top of Rae and was clumsily pulling down her pink leggings. She started to stop him, but couldn't think of a good reason to protest quick enough. She was left feeling extra horny by Prosper and figured that at that point any sex had to be better than no sex, correct? Wrong!

In true Legend fashion, he randomly stabbed at her opening without any sort of rhythm. Rae laid in her bed trying with all of her might to imagine that he was Prosper. However, the logical part of her brain knew that Prosper would never offer her any bullshit that vaguely resembled what Legend was doing.

When he finished, he went to the bathroom to discard the used condom. After he returned, Rae could see that not only was he getting dressed, but that he had an attitude. Typically, she had to put him out, but not today.

Although she truly didn't care and had an attitude of her own, she asked, "Is everything okay?"

"Yeah, I guess." He mumbled.

Shrugging her shoulders, she headed towards her bathroom and washed him off of her. When she returned to her bedroom, she was surprised to find him still sitting on the side of her bed.

Awkwardly she said, "Uhhh hello...I thought that you were leaving."

Ignoring her sarcasm, Legend replied, "You know I really liked you. I was really falling for you and now I can see that I mean nothing to you. I'm just a joke. I know that I'm not the most endowed man and I may not be a beast in the

Bedroom, but I'm a good man. I was good to you. I'm very observant and highly perceptive, did you truly think that I wouldn't notice a difference in the way your pussy feels?

The grip is different...it's off. I know that we never agreed to date exclusively, but I was under the impression that we were. I'm not even mad at you though...I'm mad at myself. I should've known better. All your excuses not to have sex with me and then there's the nigga at the restaurant.

You have feelings for him. I saw it then, but thought that the ring on his finger meant something to both of you, but apparently it doesn't. I wish you all the best Desirae." With that Legend left Desirae sitting there looking like a fool.

He had read her like a book. All she could do was knock on Zo's door, climb in his bed and cry like a big baby on his shoulder.

The next morning Zo brought his bestie breakfast in bed. He didn't bother her with questions last night, but now he needed to know what had her so upset.

"So, what brought you into my room during dick stroking hours bitch?" Zo inquired in a way that only he could.

"It's such a long story, I don't even know where to start." She chortled.

"Try at the beginning." Zo suggested.

"Well, you know that I've been crushing on Prosper for as far back as I can remember. You also know that he lives next door and the day that you got snowed in at your parents' house he came over and shoveled the driveway. I offered him a cup of hot chocolate with extra marshmallows and a seat in front of the fireplace.

Well one thing led to another and I ended up giving him

one of my infamous foot massages which led to him sucking the soul out of my Kitty. I came five times best friend! Then..." Rae trailed trying to determine if she should continue.

"Then what heifer?!" Zo exclaimed with wide eyes.

"Then we kind of had sex, but not really." She shrugged.

"What in the confused, delusional type of shit are you talking about Rae? Did you or did you not fuck him?" Zo asked for clarification.

"I don't know! He only put it in twice, so does that really count?"

"Ummm, yes bitch! It counts. But why just twice? Was your cat meowing?" Zo teased.

"No, you fucker, I keep her squeaky clean." Rae rebutted sticking her index finger into her vagina and swiping Zo's upper lip with it.

After Zo rolled around being extra and claiming that he was dying, he licked his lips, smiled and said that he might be straight after all.

∞

BANG BANG BANG!!!

"Who in the hell is it knocking like the god damn police???!!!" Zo screamed mad as hell from being awaken from his peaceful sleep.

Looking at the grandfather clock only infuriated him even further when his eyes registered that it was only one-forty-five in the morning.

Roughly swinging the front door open he sassily belted, "Honey, do you know what time it is?!"

His scowl softened once he noticed that the typically well put together woman looked frazzled and worried. He could tell that she had been crying. Before he could say anything else, the door opened wider as a concerned Rae looked at Claryssa and BJ. The toddler's head was resting on her mother's shoulder as she slept without a care in the world.

"Claryssa, is everything okay?" Rae asked guiltily. She prayed that the woman hadn't discovered her and Prosper's transgressions and was at her door to confront her.

Claryssa cried, "My husssbbbaanndd's been shhhhotttt! Prosper's been shot!"

"What?!" Both Rae and Zo yelled while clutching their imaginary pearls.

Their reactions stirred little BJ from her sleep and she soon joined her mother's tear feast.

After consoling the woman, she finally pulled herself together enough to say, "Look guys, I know that you don't know me that well, but I need a huge favor. I would really appreciate it if you could watch my daughter for me.

I do not know how my husband is doing or what to expect, but what I do know is that I do not want her to see her father laid up in a hospital bed possibly dead or dying. If it is too much, I'll understand. If you are willing, I will make sure that you are well compensated. I don't know how long I'll be there, but I really need you right now." She sobbed.

Truth be told, Rae was freaking out as much as Claryssa was, if not more. Hell, she wanted to ride with her to the damn hospital, not baby sit. Instead she remained calm as she accepted BJ and her diaper bag.

"You don't know how much I appreciate this. My contact information is in the side zipper.

Rae and Zo glanced at each other at a loss for words as they closed the door behind the woman.

# « Chapter 22 Brownie Points »

**AS PROSPER STRUGGLED** to force his heavy eyes open, he winced in pain. He felt as if he had been stoned to the brink of death. When the bright lights pierced his eyes, he immediately snapped them shut again. For a few minutes he relied on his other senses to acclimate him to his current surroundings.

The unmistakable scents infiltrated his nares while the beeping of machines told him that he was in a hospital. But why? As he thought back to earlier in the evening, he recalled spying on his neighbor, he remembered dicking his wife down and he also remembered hanging out with his cousin Charlie.

"Oh shit, Charlie!" Prosper shouted as he sat straight up before the pain knocked him back down.

As he collapsed back onto the bed, real tears streamed down his face due to the pain, but also because he didn't know if Charlie was okay or not. Soon the nurses rushed in to investigate the loud yelling coming from his room.

"Mr. Collins, please calm down before you hurt yourself. Try to relax. Someone please run and get him some Lorazepam!" An older heavyset Hispanic nurse yelled out.

"It's okay now, we are taking care of you. Can you tell me your name and date of birth?" She asked.

Prosper told her what she wanted to know. There was nothing wrong with his memory. He remembered his entire life because it had just flashed before his eyes what he thought was a few hours ago.

"My mouth is so dry and I'm so hungry. How long have I been asleep? When am I getting out of here?" Prosper asked.

"Here suck on this here. I'm Nurse Tina." She stated handing Prosper a lemon-flavored glycerin swab.

He just stared at it in her hand. What the hell was a lemon-flavored Q-tip supposed to do for his hungry ass. Plus, he wasn't in the business of sucking on shit. Popsicles and lollipops were for women.

As if reading his mind, Nurse Tina chuckled.

"Mr. Collins, you've been in a coma for nearly a week so that's why your mouth is dry and you're so hungry. I can't give you anything to eat until we notify your doctor that you're awake and she gives the orders. We have to assess your ability to swallow first." Nurse Tina elaborated.

"Woah, I've been here for a week?! What the hell? I need to get out of here, like right now. I have work to do and I can't get it done from this hospital bed." Prosper spazzed.

As he attempted to remove the tubes connected to him, his nurse stopped him.

"Look Mr. Collins, I don't want to have to place you in restraints, but I will if I have to. Oh, great here's Dr. Owens now." Nurse Tina introduced.

"Hello there. I'm so glad that you're awake. You were shot three times. Once in the left knee, and twice in your abdomen. You lost a lot of blood and went into shock. We had to give you several units of blood.

You should thank your neighbor when you're up to it, she donated some of her blood to you as well. You have a rare blood type and we were running short. We were able to repair the damage to your liver and we were also able to remove the bullets.

I think the worst of it will come from your knee. You will require some physical therapy to ensure that you get up and moving like before. You're not out of the woods yet. I still want to monitor you and run some tests on you for a few days, then and only then will I discharge you.

You have a couple of Jackson-Pratt drains coming from your abdomen. It's a closed-suction medical device that is commonly used as a post-operative drain for collecting bodily fluids from surgical sites. Be careful not to pull them out. We will assess and empty them throughout the day."

"Can I eat now?" Prosper asked overwhelmed with all of the information that had just been laid on him.

"Yes, I'm going to order you a clear liquid diet in order to give your stomach a chance to wake up. If you tolerate it, I'll remove your NG tube and advance you by supper. Any other questions?"

"Yes, actually I want to know how my cousin Charles

Stewart is doing...is he okay?" Prosper dreadfully asked.

"Hey cuzzo! I'm right here! I just went to the cafeteria to eat something. You should know by now that I'm good at playing possum! I'm not going out that easy." Charlie assured nonchalantly strolling into the hospital room.

A fresh flow of tears streamed down Prosper's face as he silently thanked God for answering his prayers. Getting shot seemed to bring out the emotional side in him. He couldn't wait for the hospital staff to leave so that they could talk privately. Unfortunately, that would have to wait as the hospital staff were ordered to perform a battery of tests on him to ensure that everything was functioning properly. He could feel his dick and that was all that mattered to him.

A few hours later, Prosper finally got to spend time alone with Charlie. He immediately started asking questions about the events that led up to him getting shot.

"Hey nigga, what was all that shit about?" Prosper whispered once the nurse closed the door behind her.

"P, you won't believe this shit man!" Charlie whispered loudly.

"Somehow, I think that I will." Prosper responded weakly.

"Well, you know how me, and you were chopping it up at the restaurant? Apparently, the brother of the nigga we robbed overheard us talking and reported back to that nigga. At least that's what the streets are saying. Also, when they were popping off at us, I heard one of them niggas yelling about us robbing them and shit." Charlie quickly rambled in one breath.

Prosper rubbed his goatee as if in deep thought before quickly yelling out, "Oh shit! Rae and her brothers!"

"What? What about them?" A puzzled Charlie inquired.

"We mentioned them at your spot that day, so if they heard our entire dialogue then they probably heard the part about her brothers taking the work too. I have to let her know ASAP!"

"She's been keeping BJ while Claryssa comes to visit you every day. After Claryssa picks her up, then "Megan" comes up here to check on you herself." Charlie stated shocking Prosper.

"Yo, seriously? *Rae* comes up here every day to see a nigga?" Prosper replied ignoring the fact that Claryssa came every day as well. Hell, she was his wife, she was obligated to check on his ass.

"Yeah man. She comes up every day after Claryssa picks up BJ." Charlie repeated.

A huge smile spread across Prosper's face. Not only had Rae been checking up on him and donating blood, but she was also spending time with and getting to know BJ better. She had scored more brownie points with Prosper than either of them realized.

# « Chapter 23 Guilt By Association »

LATER THAT EVENING Rae had just finished giving BJ her bath and was about to tuck her in when she heard knocking on the door. She was surprised to find Claryssa standing there so early. Normally, she'd be gone for a few hours, but not today. Without asking any questions, Rae went to get a sleeping BJ and handed her to her mother. She was growing fonder and more attached to the toddler with each passing day.

It was amazing to see how much BJ and Rae's relationship had evolved in such a short period of time. When Rae had started watching her in the evenings, she was initially extremely shy and timid. Luckily, she soon warmed up to Rae and she beamed in her presence whenever her mom dropped her off.

Once Rae shut the door, she rushed upstairs to get

herself together. Even though Prosper was still unconscious, she still took extra time to make herself presentable every evening. Since Claryssa had returned home so early, Rae decided to take herself a nice warm bubble bath. She had had a long stressful day at school and needed to unwind for a bit. Once her bath water started to get cold, she decided to wrap up her shower and make her way to the hospital.

It was the typical cool winter night that kept most Texans in the house if they could help it. Her mind was so preoccupied with school, exams, work and Prosper that she hadn't even noticed the dark vehicle that trailed behind her as soon as she exited her driveway. One left turn turned into two which was then followed by a right.

Imagine Rae's surprise when she was violently rear ended a mere mile away from her destination. The unexpected collision nearly sent her into cardiac arrest as she screamed and struggled to regain control of her vehicle. Her car had sent her into oncoming traffic, but she was able to maneuver her battered car back into its correct lane.

Breathing heavily, Rae looked into her rearview mirror and spotted a black unknown car quickly approaching her vehicle. It was too dark out for her to attempt to see who was driving the car as she pressed her foot down on the gas, hoping to avoid being hit again.

It didn't take long for a few good Samaritans to pull over and offer assistance. Within minutes she could hear sirens as they quickly made their way towards her. Although Rae was awake and wanted to reach for her phone to alert her family of the incident, she didn't know the extent of her injuries, so she decided to remain still.

Once the paramedics came, she answered as many of their questions as she could. She was encouraged to stay up and talk to them. They were afraid to allow her to close her eyes, but soon she felt herself struggling to listen to their commands. There were just too many faces, voices and lights surrounding her. As she drifted further and further into darkness.

It wasn't until a few hours later that she found herself trying to force her eyes open. An uneasy feeling swept over her because she felt as if she was being watched. Cautiously opening her eyes, she burst into tears when her mother's worried face came into view on the right of her. Her mom looked pleasantly surprised to see that her battered daughter was now awake.

Rae then noticed her dad and brothers sitting at her bedside as well. She internally thanked God for being alive. After the doctors and nurses came in and notified her that aside from a concussion, hematoma to her forehead and a nasty black eye, she was virtually unscathed. The CT scan of her head showed no bleeding. They were going to keep her overnight for monitoring, but were confident that she'd be discharged the next day.

After Rae pleaded with her parents to go home and get some rest, they finally left for their home. Rae wasn't completely sure why, but she had told everyone that she couldn't remember what had happened prior to the accident.

Statements were obtained at the scene and the eyewitnesses had told the police that she was rear ended by a black car. She didn't want to scare her parents, so she decided to pretend as if the heinous act was random. She thought it was odd that her brothers lagged behind.

Rae's brothers remained silent and stoic, however after a few moments she noticed that Ant was texting. She wanted them to leave as well, so that she could be alone. Just as she was about to throw them out, her hospital room door opened, and her heart leapt into her throat when she saw Prosper being wheeled into her room by a guy she'd never seen before.

Prosper's eyes locked in on Rae and she could tell that he was angry. It wasn't until he was pushed over towards her brothers that he finally diverted his attention to them and dapped them up.

"Sup Ant. Sup Sam. Hey, this is my cuz Charlie. Charlie these are the clients I told you about before and their sister Desirae." Prosper introduced.

After the pleasantries were out of the way, Prosper continued, "Me and my cousin were sneaking down to the cafeteria when I saw Desirae being rolled in on a stretcher. She wasn't moving man and I didn't know what was wrong with her, but it didn't look good.

We tried to follow her, but they stopped us and ratted me out to my nurse who came and brought me back up to my floor. I can't seem to shake that heifer! Damn!" He explained looking around in a paranoid manner.

"Anyway, that's when I hit yall up." Prosper said.

Sam remained quiet, however, he nodded his head in approval while Ant said, "Thanks bro, good looking out. We still don't know what's going on, but I know Rae enough to know that she isn't being forthcoming." He stated glaring at his little sister.

Rae gave them a weak smile and shrugged her shoulders. She wanted to smack them for talking about her as if she wasn't lying there just a few feet away.

Prosper's face suddenly turned extremely serious as his eyes focused on Rae again.

He then said, "I think that I may know who is responsible for causing her accident."

"What?! Who?!" All three siblings shouted louder than they intended to.

"Long story short, remember that bag that I left in your car a few years ago from the robbery me and Charlie did?" Prosper asked Rae and she quickly nodded.

"Well me and Charlie recently made the stupid mistake of discussing it in his restaurant about a week ago without paying close attention to our surroundings. Apparently, we were overheard discussing details of the robbery by that nigga's people. The three of you were briefly mentioned, so that makes me believe that Desirae was targeted by those fools too." Prosper explained.

"What do you mean, too?" Sam finally spoke up.

"Those punk muthafuckas shot my cousin up the same night that they overheard us conversing and he's been unconscious since. Hell, he just woke up today." Charlie elaborated in a frustrated manner.

"Shit!" Ant shouted.

"Fuck!" Sam yelled.

"Damn!" Rae groaned.

If the entire situation wasn't so serious, all of them most likely would've found humor in the siblings' defeated responses.

After the fact that all of their lives were still in grave jeopardy sank in for a few moments, Prosper finally said, "Man we have to take care of those fools before they come after us again. I have a wife and a seed out here, not to mention my little sister. I don't know what they know about us, but I'm damn sure not about to be a sitting duck out here.

I know that they know by now that I'm still breathing and it's only a matter of time before the news makes them aware that the hit on Desirae failed as well. Fuck that, niggas lets go!" Prosper shouted getting himself worked up.

Desirae was a little salty at the mention of his wife, but his bravery did make her nipples protrude in her hospital gown just a little. Not wanting anyone to notice, she pulled her thin sheet up to her neck. Even sitting in a wheelchair with a cast on his leg, Prosper was one of the most beautiful men that her eyes had ever seen.

She chuckled softly when she noticed that his cousin mushed him in the head when he attempted to get his decrepit ass up to walk on his fractured extremity. Deep in her nasty thoughts she had tuned out their verbal exchanges, however when her two brothers leaned down and kissed her on the forehead and Prosper's cousin waved her goodbye, she knew that the three of them were about to finish the war that had been started years ago.

Her hit and run had been all over the news, however her name was not disclosed. Afrika as it turned out was pregnant by Sam and he told Rae that he didn't tell her about the accident to avoid her stressing out. Rae intentionally avoided telling Zo as well.

She didn't want her best friends to know until they absolutely needed to and hopefully by that time everyone would be out of harm's way. Charlie had guys from around the way anonymously protecting their close friends and family members while they avenged both Rae and Prosper. Charlie felt fully responsible for everything since it was after all, his bright idea when they were teenagers. That night, they painted the city crimson.

# « Chapter 24 Side Chicks Wear Capes Too »

"**WHAT ARE YOU STARING** at?" Prosper asked sleepily later that night.

"I wasn't staring at anything or anyone, you just happened to wake up as I glanced at you." Rae shot back embarrassed that her eye didn't move quicker to avoid their current awkward conversation.

"Mhmmmm..." Prosper hummed sexily with his eyes sitting low.

"Damn, he's fine!" Rae thought, but unfortunately for her, her thoughts were sometimes involuntarily spoken out loud.

Sometimes, she didn't even realize that it happened until the people around her reacted.

At first, she didn't think anything about it until Prosper chuckled and cockily thanked her. Clasping both hands across her deceptive mouth, she tried to crawl inside of the ultra-thin hospital mattress.

Prosper couldn't help but think about how gorgeous Desirae still was, even with the black eye and lump on her head. The sight of her injuries infuriated him and to make matters worse, his injuries prevented him from causing harm to those who had caused harm to them.

Deciding not to tease an already mortified Desirae, he rolled over to her bed and tapped her shoulder. She ignored him at first, she was still praying that she would suddenly become invisible without any luck.

After Prosper continued to annoy her, she finally replied, "Why are you still in here? Don't you have your own room two floors from here? You know your nurse is going to kick your ass for disappearing again."

Prosper shuddered at the mention of his mean nurse, however, luckily for him, he now had a younger and nicer nurse who wasn't on his ass as much as the older Hispanic lady. He guessed that the old broad was hibernating upside down in some dark cave that day.

"I'm keeping an eye on you until I receive confirmation that those niggas have been dealt with." Prosper said.

"An *eye* on *me*?! You've been snoring your ass off for the past four hours! I've been watching you living your best life in la la land. Oh, let me guess, you were going to make our attackers slip in the drool puddle that you left over on my bedside table." Rae joked.

Prosper laughed and said, "Hey heifer, I meant well. I told Nurse Ratchet not to give me anything to make me sleepy, but I think that heifer roofied my ass! She has probably been taking advantage of me in my sleep the whole week I've been out!"

Rae burst out laughing finally becoming more at ease since her slip up.

"You are so ridiculous." She giggled.

"And you are so beautiful." He countered seriously.

Blushing under his intense gaze, the butterflies in Rae's stomach fluttered so strongly that the hair on her body stood erect.

Prosper couldn't get up from his wheelchair, so he beckoned Rae to get up on the side of her bed. She did as he had asked and made her way to the right side of her bed. While he stared up at her from his chair, she stared self-consciously down into her lap. Sitting in front of Prosper, the guy who she had always been attracted to made her feel like the insecure girl she used to be back in high school. Her facial injuries weren't exactly a confidence booster.

Even at her most obese moments, she could always count on her flawless face, but not that day.

Prosper being the perceptive guy that he was, picked up on her body language and said, "Bring your sexy ass over here and kiss me Desirae."

A small smile formed around her mouth as she skeptically swept her eyes across his face. Prosper was two seconds away from repeating himself when Rae slowly stood to her feet. He had parked his wheelchair so close to her bed that no additional steps were needed to close the gap between them.

"I see someone has difficulty following directions." Prosper whispered as he pulled Rae's hand down so that their lips could finally meet.

Once their lips touched, electricity instantly circulated throughout their erroneous zones. The fact that neither of them had brushed their teeth in recent hours never even crossed their minds as their tongues sensually danced with one another. It was almost as if their tongues were competing in an erotic dance.

Rae's clit throbbed as her pussy sprung a leak. Her engorged nipples once again fought against the material of her gown and this time they didn't go unnoticed.

Prosper's hands both went under her gown and rolled, squeezed and tweaked her chocolate Hershey kisses. Sexy moans escaped her throat as she subconsciously squeezed and gyrated her hips as if she were riding an imaginary dick.

Prosper's dick was beyond hard as he popped a titty into his mouth and slipped two fingers into Rae's snug tunnel. He knew that with his abdominal wounds and broken leg that he couldn't fuck her, however the feel and smell of her was making him want to die trying.

After cumming on Prosper's fingers and watching him lick them clean, Rae lifted up Prosper's gown and consumed his member up in one swift motion. Prosper hissed at the euphoria her technique gave him. He was very vocal about how well she was satisfying him, and his acoustics made her try even harder to please him. She wanted to give him the best blow job of his life so that he'd never be able to live happily ever after with his beloved wife.

Rae wanted him to crave her and no one else. There was so much purpose, love and thought behind each massage her

SHEENA PERRY

esophagus delivered to the tip of his meaty member. Gagging and cuteness were non-factors that fateful morning. Spit was not only running down her chin and neck, but even her breasts was saturated through her gown. He was too good for lazy ass standing head or squatting head. No! Rae dropped down to her knees on the hospital floor that day. She was no nasty bitch, so she did throw a soaker pad down first.

Side chicks all over the world were standing proudly with their chests puffed out and SC capes on. She never cared much for giving head in the past, but she could honestly say that she thoroughly enjoyed blessing Prosper with some good neck. Prosper had to snatch his wood from Rae several times to keep from cumming. He didn't want it to ever end.

He suddenly had the overpowering urge to feel her. He knew that he'd have to be careful with his wounds, but he needed to be inside of her.

Grabbing her face softly he whispered, "Turn around and just sit on it."

"Yes daddy." She said cockily wiping her juicy lips off on her gown.

Rae stood to her feet, grabbed Prosper's dick and placed it at her entrance. She bit her lip and gently gyrated her hips in a circular motion to get his oversized erection past her resistance. It drove him crazy that he couldn't thrust upwards like he wanted to. All he could do was sit back and enjoy the ride.

Once Rae worked his tool completely inside of her, she sat stagnant for a few moments while she adjusted to his size. She liked that he had no qualms about letting her know that her coochie was fire. She then began rubbing on her clit and squeezing her pussy muscles tightly around Prosper.

Rae came time and time again coating Prosper's dick with her juices. When Prosper had had enough, he gripped her hips and slowly began to guide her up and down on his dick. They were both moaning as if they were in a hotel room instead of a hospital room. Neither tried to silence the other.

Perspiration covered their battered faces and bodies as they continued to imprint on one another. Soon Rae felt Prosper's body stiffened as he firmly pinned her hips in place before convulsing below her. She knew that he was coming inside of her, but his grip was too strong to escape, and she was too weak to protest as he squirted his semen deep inside of her unprotected womb.

Before an exhausted Rae could stand to her feet and with Prosper's still erect dick holding her sticky pussy hostage, the pair nearly shit on themselves when in walks her doctor, parents, brothers and a lone smiling Charlie.

# « Chapter 25 Her Man Is My Man »

"**HEY, MAN! WHAT THE** fuck?!!!" Ant charged towards the pair so that he could fight Prosper.

Sam and Charlie fought hard to keep him back while a scared and humiliated Rae fixed her gown and stood up to get off of Prosper. The loud wet noises of Prosper's now softening dick echoed through the room and gave the room a show as her vagina regurgitated his penis and semen onto his already shiny dick. He tried desperately to hide himself, however the angle of his chair to the door didn't offer much of a blind spot.

Rae's father and brothers departed first, however, her mother angrily glared at her only daughter for a few moments. Through clenched teeth she stated, "I came here to see how you

THE WHORE NEXT DOOR

were feeling. I suppose you are feeling good. Very good in fact. Your father and I raised you better than this Desirae Marie! I never in a million years would have imagined that you would mess around with a married man. Your neighbor's man at that! You've just become a regular whore next door, haven't you?!"

All of her mother's words had hurt Rae because it was all true, but the last sentence cut her to the core. Additionally, Valentina had used her middle name. That's when Rae knew shit was serious. Her mother had always been saucy and never held her tongue and Rae typically appreciated that quality in her.

That day she just wished that her mother's fury was directed towards someone else. While she was sexing Prosper, she knew that she'd regret it, however, she never thought that she'd live to regret her decision so soon.

With her head held lower than the earth's crust, tears violated her warm cheeks. She hated disappointing her family, especially her mother.

She of all people had witnessed firsthand how her dad's extramarital affairs wreaked havoc on her mother's sanity as they were growing up. What many people didn't know was that they had actually separated and were living as roommates for the better part of two years before a desperate and heartbroken James was able to convince Valentina to at least consider taking him back.

Valentina loved her husband dearly and had always dreamt of raising her children up in a two-parent home just as she had been, however, she refused to continue to allow her children to see her play Boo Boo the Fool any longer. She had instilled in her daughter how much home wreckers ruined families and that they should all have bleach poured into their toxic wombs.

The yearlong separation had been a frightening wake up call for him. He had never loved any of the women he'd had sex with. Although initially flattered, he eventually grew to hate how much women threw themselves at him solely based on his good looks and the fact that he was a successful dentist.

In the beginning he was able to fight the temptation and wave them off, but after a while he begin to believe the hype. He had made the mistake of forgetting the strength that laid within the beautiful woman that he had married. All of his little conquests had given him a God complex and somewhere along the way he thought that Valentina would always be there through all of his bullshit.

Valentina knew that her marriage was nearing its expiration date, however it was the raging bout of Chlamydia that sent her over the edge. Every time she thought about the humiliation and discomfort that she endured regarding that entire incident caused her to be rageful. She couldn't help but to think about how easily the chlamydia that he had transmitted to her could've as easily been HIV. She could've kicked her own ass for assuming that he was at least being safe with his whores.

She filed for divorce and requested a legal separation prior to even finishing her course of antibiotics to rid her of her chlamydial infection. James had taken it way too far now. Through her anger, Valentina couldn't fathom any thoughts of reconciling with her philandering husband.

She was perfectly fine with co-parenting and cohabitating the same living quarters. She loved the hell out of their family house and had no intentions of ever leaving. She knew that he felt the same way and that was a huge reason why she didn't force his ass out of the house altogether. Plus, she didn't want her children to suffer.

Unlike her, James didn't grow up with both parents in

the house. They made a pact that should they ever split up; they'd keep things amicable despite the circumstances. Working and living with an estranged husband was no easy feat, however, Valentina continued on with business as usual. Once she removed her wedding ring, male suitors pursued the young gorgeous dentist relentlessly. It drove James absolutely crazy.

Flowers and candy were being delivered on a daily basis. Valentina even went on a few dates, which infuriated James. In the end she realized that a man wasn't what she needed. She needed to work on reacquainting herself with herself. James also needed to reacquaint himself with the woman whom he married. After hundreds of pleas, tears, money, promises, trips, and sorrys, Valentina eventually agreed to go on a date with her husband.

She wanted them to literally start over from scratch. He courted her as if his life depended on it. After their tenth successful date she told James that they both needed to attend marital counseling. He wasn't crazy about that notion because he knew in his heart of hearts that he would never jeopardize their marriage or lives again playing the field. At any rate, there was literally nothing that he wouldn't have agreed to in order to restore his broken family.

She made him wait an additional year before she even allowed her husband to sniff her cooter and that was only after he was tested for every organism detectable via a microscope. Her PTSD from being burned all those years ago still had her making James glove up before they made love. The day that he'd burned her was the last day he'd ever felt his wife's kitty in its natural state.

As frustrating as it was to him, he understood. Hell, had the tables been turned and she had burned him, he'd be in prison for murder. He knew that he had no right to demand anything of her. He went with the well-deserved punches and thanked the good Lord above each day for his Queen. He was aware that Valentina could've left him after all of their children left the nest, yet the fact that she chose to stay showed that she truly did love him.

All of those factors are what made Valentina so furious with her foolish daughter. Her daughter could have any man that she wanted, yet she was playing second fiddle to someone else's man. She could just wring her neck! After stating her peace, Valentina walked out of the hospital room deciding that her daughter needed a dose of tough love. As Rae continued to cry, Prosper was at a loss as to what to do. He wanted to comfort Desirae, however, he didn't want to trigger her.

Charlie stayed in the room as well and still sported his stupid grin. He was happy as hell that his cousin had finally hooked up with the pretty woman. He could tell that his cousin was truly feeling her. Charlie had never liked Prosper's wife anyway.

Prosper finally decided to throw caution to the wind and reached out to Rae. Rae's body jerked back so quickly that she appeared to be repulsed.

"Don't touch me!" Rae snapped.

Prosper would probably never admit it, but his feelings were genuinely hurt. One minute he was rearranging her organs with his dick, but now he couldn't even lay a comforting hand on her shoulder.

"My bad I..." Prosper started but was interrupted.

"You know what? Save it. None of it even matters. Can you please just get out?! You've done quite enough." Rae belted in between sobs.

Feeling hurt and defeated Prosper motioned for Charlie to come and push him back to his room.

As he was pushed over the threshold, he turned his head to look at Rae and said, "I'm not sure what all of this shit means, but what I know is that you're gonna be mine one day."

With that, the two men were gone, leaving Rae with her thoughts and a heavy heart.

## « Chapter 26 Stepping Back »

"**OH MY GOD BABY!!!** When did you wake up?!" Claryssa exclaimed excitedly as she walked into Prosper's hospital room to find him very much awake.

Before he could even answer her, she fired another question his way, "Why didn't you call me? I would've come sooner. Plus, I would've brought BJ. She's been asking me where you are nearly every second of every day."

Prosper felt terrible at the mention of his daughter missing him. He had come incredibly close to never seeing his daughter again. Tears spilled from his wife's eyes causing his heart to break a little. He hated to see her cry especially when he was the source of her pain.

Attempting to lighten the mood a little he said, "I am

looking kind of busted and was hoping to get my haircut before you came up to see me, but I guess you've already been up here seeing me look a mess anyway. Where's my baby girl at though?"

"She's over at the neighbor's house with Zo. I have been letting her stay with Desirae in the evenings whenever I come up to see you, but she wasn't there today." Claryssa shrugged.

Prosper had nothing against Zo or his sexuality, however, he didn't feel comfortable with his daughter being left with him. He didn't know him like that and trusted no man besides Charlie. He also pondered if he should reveal what had happened to Desirae the previous evening.

After a few moments of contemplation, he decided not to alarm her with it. He didn't want her to grow paranoid since the problems had been eliminated. They were all now safe to resume their lives as they knew it.

"Hey babe. I appreciate you for holding shit down while I've been in here and also for coming up to see my ugly ass every day, but I don't know that nigga Zo like that. Go pick her back up and don't drop her off over there anymore, unless Desirae is there." Prosper stated in a serious tone.

"P, now you know that I wouldn't have left our baby there if I felt that she was endangered. Don't even come at me like that. Besides you don't know Desirae any more than you know Zo." She countered in an offended manner.

Deciding to soften his tone and save face he said, "Yeah, you're right. Well, can you please pick her up and bring her up here so that I can see her. I miss her little bad ass. I miss you too." He actually did.

He knew that his first approach had only made his wife defensive, but now she was smiling and ready to do what she had originally been asked to do.

The next day, a couple of floors down, Rae had finally called her besties up and told them what had happened to her. She was no fool. She had told Zo first and he cursed her the hell out. After he cooled down a little and was sure that Rae was safe, they both devised a plan to let a pregnant Afrika know.

Zo was tasked with picking Afrika up. He had blind folded her, put ear protectors in her ears and rubbed vapor rub under her nose in an attempt to hide the fact that they were going to a hospital. They didn't want her rushing alone to the hospital in a panic. Afrika would have to see firsthand that her friend was okay, so that's what they arranged.

Zo led Afrika right up to Rae's hospital bed. He then removed her ear protectors and her mask. Her eyes immediately widened and filled with tears once her eyes focused on Rae's bruised and swollen face. Rae wasted no time embracing her friend and telling her what had happened to her. Naturally Afrika was just as upset as Zo had been, but she understood why Rae had handled everything as cautiously as she had.

With all of her tests coming back negative, Rae was able to go home two evenings after her accident. Luckily, she worked for her family, so they understood her circumstances. She was already ahead in her classes, so she wasn't missing anything there either. She just wanted to go home and relax in her own bed.

She wanted the accident and her affair with Prosper to disappear. She was avoiding her mother since she had chewed her a new asshole. How could she face her after that? Rae had become the type of woman that her mother despised the most.

After kicking Prosper out of her hospital room, he made no further attempts to visit her. Although she was relieved, she just couldn't shake the small twinge of disappointment she felt leaving without so much as a goodbye from him. She knew that Claryssa had stopped leaving BJ with Zo in the evenings, so she assumed that they were all one big happy family again.

She needed to move on from her short-lived romance. What did she expect to manifest from it anyway? She knew that the likelihood of Prosper leaving Claryssa for her was a long shot. Hell, did she really want him to leave her and their daughter for her? She was so conflicted. She wanted him more than anything she'd ever wanted before in her life, but without the devastation that their union was sure to cause.

When she returned home, it was back to business as usual for both of them. The first order of business for Rae was getting a new car. Her car had been totaled and it broke her heart. She loved that car. As her car salesmen walked her onto their showroom, Rae fell in love with the courlis red 2021 Infinity Limited QX80. Once her hazel orbs fixated on the red beauty, all of the other cars disappeared. The salesman was happier because he could save his corny sales pitch.

Months passed and before she knew it, summer was in full bloom. That summer marked the beginning of what felt like a nightmare.

# « Chapter 27 Intellectually Interrupted »

"HEY MA. HEY DAD." Rae called out as she entered her parents' home.

They were throwing their infamous neighborhood summer barbecue, and all were welcome to attend.

She sported a cute peach colored backless dress that hugged her slim waist snuggly while the hip area flared out exaggeratedly. Her body looked so perfect in that dress that she nearly looked unreal. Many women paid thousands of dollars on cosmetics surgeries, yet still held no candle to her.

She was naturally beautiful. Her hair was bone straight and the ends were so long that they caressed the top of her ass cheeks. For the most part she swept her long mane over her right shoulder and allowed it to drape over the front of her. She knew that she'd be walking around a lot, so she rocked a pair of cute brown Jessica Simpson sandals. Her finger and toenails were painted the same peach as her dress. Large hoop earrings and a beat face completed her ensemble.

Rae had been dating a gym teacher who Zo introduced her to named Dex. Dex was a cutie with a nice physique. He was medium brown and about six foot three with a muscular build. Rae often teased Dex about how she wished that her high school gym teachers looked like him.

He had full kissable lips that she loved nibbling on. Dex was twenty-five, single, straight, had a good job, had a vehicle, had an apartment, decent credit and no children. The sex was nice too. What more could a woman ask for?

Dex was scheduled to stop by the barbecue later in the day. Although they had only been dating for a little over a month, Rae decided that she liked him enough to introduce him to her family. They spent virtually every available moment they had together, and life was just too short to be moving at a snail's pace.

Rae couldn't even front, she gave Dex the cookie on their first date. She figured that they were both grown, so why play cat and mouse when it was something that they both obviously wanted. He was no Prosper by any means; however, he was a complete upgrade from Legend's non-stroke having ass.

While a lot of the party goers including Afrika and Zo were out in the back enjoying the pool, Rae was in the kitchen sneaking a corner of her mother's infamous macaroni and cheese. As usual, she was caught red handed. Her mother had eyes everywhere when it came to her children fiddling with her pots and pans.

Rae had a goofy smirk on her face as she tried her

darndest not to chew the piping hot, yet delicious bite that was marinating on her heightened taste buds. The Styrofoam container that housed her swiped food was resting behind her in an effort to elude the wise woman. Valentina just shook her head exposing her stark white teeth.

"You and your intellectually interrupted brothers never could wait until the food was finished to eat. If you're not careful, you're going to start putting back on some of that weight." She teased her daughter.

Rae felt a little self-conscious because although she was still toned and fabulous, her cute clothes were fitting a little snugger than she was used to these days. Sensing her daughter's insecurities, she said, "La hija, eat your food," and winked at her daughter.

As Valentina was about to exit the kitchen to rejoin the guest outside Rae blurred out, "I really am sorry for everything, mom. I never meant to hurt and embarrass you when I... well you know."

For some reason, no matter how old Rae was, she always resorted to a child in her mother's presence when she knew that she had disappointed her. She felt bashful and foolish all over again.

Valentina walked over to her daughter and said, "My love, you and I both know that the best apology is changed behavior. We have discussed that matter ad nauseam and from what I see, you've done just that. I will not always like the decisions that you and your watermelon head brothers make, but I'll always love you. I've already forgiven you Bonita and now it's time that you forgave yourself."

Valentina then turned and left leaving her words to soak in. Rae eventually finished her plate of stolen food and joined the party. Walking out onto the beautiful deck, she smiled at the comradery she saw amongst the people who were present.

She soon heard, "Desirae, is that you?" From behind her.

Spinning around to find the voice, her mouth dropped when she saw Claryssa standing there with BJ and sexy ass Prosper. They both looked genuinely surprised to see Rae. Who the hell had invited them? They always seemed to crash parties making shit awkward.

Snapping out of her thoughts she walked towards the trio and greeted them all with a warm hug. When she hugged Prosper, his bold ass discreetly licked her neck before releasing her. She internally prayed and willed her body not to react to that man.

Luckily for her, just at that moment Dex approached them and introduced himself as Rae's man. Her face lit up because they had never officially given one another titles before. It felt great to be spoken for. The look on Prosper's face was priceless. Jealousy was written all over his face, however, none of that mattered. Hell, he was standing next to his family.

"So, Desirae and Dex, how did you two hear about this party?" Claryssa asked.

Dex took the liberty of answering for Rae when he chuckled, "This is her folks house."

Both Prosper and Claryssa's eyes widened in surprise.

"Wow, we had no idea." The marital duo spoke in unison.

Everyone was quiet for a few moments until Rae replied, "Well I'm happy that the three of you came. You all look great. Prosper, it's remarkable to see you healing up nicely. You've finally ditched the crutches I see."

Rae eye raped the man that should've been her husband. Why was that man so fine?!

"Thank you, Desirae. A client of ours invited us here and I'm happy he did. It hasn't been an easy recovery, but I'm just so grateful to still be here. God is so good." Prosper replied pulling Rae's gaze from his third leg up to his face.

Simply smiling, Rae pointed the small family over towards the activities and food. She then sought out her own family so that she could introduce her new man. Everyone loved Dex, including her overprotective brothers which surprised both Rae and Valentina. Both Zo and Afrika had already met and loved Dex for their bestie. Rae had finally revealed her affair with them both, so they were happy as hell that Dex came along.

They didn't have any issues with Prosper as a man, however, the fact that he was married with a child meant that he was not an option for Rae. Rae deserved better and they felt that Dex was clearly the better choice in the entire scenario.

Rae and Dex spent the day eating, drinking alcohol, dancing and thoroughly enjoying themselves until he had to leave early and pick up his mom from the airport. The fact that Prosper's eyes remained glued to Rae hadn't gone unnoticed by her. She did her best to behave unaffected, but internally her insides summersaulted each time she glanced his way and he was looking at her.

She certainly showed his ass no mercy and teased the hell out of him from across the yard. The alcohol had her feeling loose and brazen. Afrika was the second to leave. Sam told everyone that his son needed his rest. Afrika was all belly and her baby bump was so adorable.

Rae couldn't wait to meet her nephew. Seeing Sam so loving and overprotective of her best friend made her heart melt. Afrika had gone from being teased when they were younger to having her own salon and being relationship goals.

Rae and Zo hadn't been quite so lucky in love. Zo dated sporadically, but most of the men turned out to be assholes. Zo often had his heartbroken because for some odd reason he was attracted primarily to straight men. He dangerously tested boundaries and while he'd occasionally struck browned gold, he had received some severe ass whoopings from men who took offense to his advances.

Zo never brought any of the guys to the home that he shared with Rae just in case they wanted to start some shit. At the barbecue she smiled as she observed a fine ass guy hitting on her handsome friend. They looked great together and Rae hoped that things between the two could grow into something beyond the bedroom.

Although Rae rode to the barbecue with Zo, she told him to go ahead with his new friend. Batting her drunken eyes over at the man who had been eye fucking her all night, she knew exactly who would be giving her a ride that night.

## « Chapter 28  1 + 1 = 3 »

"**WHAT THE HELL WAS** that?!" A startled Rae sat up and shrieked noting that it was only two in the morning.

She was still quite tipsy and was unsure if she had truly heard anything or if the alcohol had her acting crazy. After listening for a few moments and not hearing anything, she'd concluded that she must've been hearing things and laid back down and dozed off.

At some point her eyes again opened and widened when she saw Prosper standing before her. He was nude and was climbing in between her thick thighs. She remembered that she had given them the code to her house in case of emergencies, so that explained how he had gotten in.

Rae made no attempts to protest when she felt her

panties sliding down over her plump ass, her legs and then her ankles. Somewhere in her drunken fog her conscious was pleading with her to not backtrack and sex Prosper again. However, a lot of blood had drained from her head and relocated to her swollen clit. Her clit was begging to be suckled and Prosper wasted no time fulfilling that need.

Rae cried out loud as Prosper made her fall in love with him all over again. She grinded upwards onto his face until he got up and slammed into her. She wasn't sure if Zo had made it back home, but in that moment she didn't care.

Prosper was beating up against the bottom of her pussy causing her legs to go numb. Tears involuntarily ran down her cheeks because she'd never felt so much pleasure in her entire life. With each rough stroke, Prosper stimulated parts of her that had never been touched before.

He kissed away her tears and asked her, "Who the fuck was that lame? That ugly ass nigga? His face looked like a collection of spare parts!" Prosper clowned jealously.

"Uhhhh! You heard him...ahhhhh! He's my man! Fuuuccckkkkk!" She belted in between moans.

"Naw baby. You need to dead that shit. Call him up right now and end that shit right now." Prosper ordered seriously with closed eyes.

Although his breathing was labored, he talked calmly through his strokes.

Thinking that he was joking, she laughed.

Her laughing at him caused Prosper to become annoyed so he sped up the pounding that he was delivering to Rae's pussy. Her eyes rolled to the back of her head as she felt herself squirting all over the both of them. A loud scream escaped from her mouth as a fresh flow of tears washed over her face.

"What are you doing to me, Prosper? What are you doing to me?!" She sobbed as he continued rotating his hips into her center.

He withdrew from her and kissed her lips before reaching over and grabbing her phone off her nightstand. He handed her the phone and repeated, "Dead that shit."

He then reinserted himself inside of her gushy stuff and pounded ferociously.

Still getting her coochie busted down, she reluctantly took the phone. Unlocking it, she called Dex. It rang several times and just as she was about to hang up, her call was picked up.

"Hello?" Rae moaned into the receiver.

Instead of hearing Dex, she heard what sounded like serious fucking going on.

"Hello?" She now called out angrily.

Again, more sex noises. Then all of the sudden she heard a familiar masculine voice call out, "Fuck yes zaddy! Fuck this bussy! I love you Dex! I love you boy!!!"

Not wanting to hear anymore, Rae hung up and looked up at a confused Prosper.

"Don't worry, it's over. He actually beat me to the punch. Now, you need to leave your wife!" Rae demanded.

"Plan is already in motion sweetheart. Trust and believe that." A sweaty Prosper assured her.

Just as Prosper went to deliver his next deep stroke Rae

let out a piercing, painful cry which caused him to immediately withdraw from her body. When he did, to his horror he noticed that blood was on his penis and on the sheet beneath Rae. Panicking he quickly picked her up, grabbed her car keys and drove her off to the nearest hospital.

"Prosper, where the hell are you?! What time did you leave here?!" A pissed Claryssa screamed into the phone.

The two of them had had an important meeting at eight in the morning, yet her husband was nowhere to be found. It wasn't like Prosper to miss important deadlines and meetings. Here it was almost eleven in the morning, and he just now nonchalantly answered his phone as if shit was sweet.

"Look, it's been a long night and a long day. We will talk about the shit when I get home. Did you reschedule our meeting?" Prosper asked calmly.

"Who is she, P? Who is the bitch that has you sneaking out and missing out on major money? The pussy must be golden because you've never missed shit on my behalf." Claryssa snapped sounding hurt.

"Look, now isn't the time or the place. We will talk when I get home. I'll see you later." Prosper said before hanging up and turning off his phone.

Turning back around to face a sleeping Rae, he'd be lying if he said that he wasn't nervous. He wanted to be with her more than anything, but worried that Claryssa would make his life hell. Once they reached the hospital, he had lied and told the hospital staff that he was Desirae's husband. He was then informed that she was four months pregnant.

Between the alcohol and medicine that she'd received, Rae had been asleep throughout the entire time. She didn't even know that she was pregnant yet...at least he didn't think so. Prosper was honest about the rough sex that they'd both had and worried that he had caused her to miscarry. When the ultrasound was performed and he heard the strong heartbeat, he cried like a baby. He was no idiot; he had already done the math and knew that the child that Rae was carrying was his. But did she know that she was pregnant? If so, why hadn't she told him.

He was even able to charm the staff into telling him that they were expecting a baby boy. He already had the name picked out and everything. Finding out about Rae's pregnancy was a game changer. There was no way that he was going to allow her to raise their baby alone.

"Owww! What the hell happened?! Why am I here? Why are you here with me?" Rae asked groggily while holding her head in pain.

"Whoa! Hold on let me help you sit up." Prosper ran over to help her.

"Were we in an accident or something? I could've sworn that I made it home and showered. I guess I didn't. How bad was it? Is everyone involved okay?" Rae panicked.

"Relax. Just try to relax. What I'm about to tell you is going to be hard to believe, but believe it."

"I came over to your house around two in the morning. Believe me when I say I tried to fight the urge to. I tried to be respectful and keep my distance. I know you deserve better than to be sneaking around with some married dude, but I just couldn't help myself after seeing you yesterday." Prosper admitted.

"You're sounding like an out of control pervert right now, but proceed." Rae pointed out.

Rae's statement had Prosper wondering if he should even continue on with his story since it was kind of borderline perverted.

Still he decided to continue, "I came into your room and we started making love. Naw, I won't even lie…we straight up started fucking. It was the best sex that either of us had ever had in our lives. You came and squirted so much that I lost cou…"

Embarrassed, Rae stated, "First of all, you cannot speak for me. I've probably had way better than you. Secondly, why don't I remember any of this bomb sex???"

"Probably because your ass was tore up last night! Anyway, I was giving you the best dick of your life when you started bleeding and screaming out in pain. I immediately picked you up and brought you in here." Prosper elaborated.

Rae gasped.

"So, what happened? What did they say is wrong with me?!" She asked worriedly.

Prosper could tell from her reaction that she genuinely didn't know about her pregnancy.

"Well, as it turns out, you're pregnant. Luckily the rough sex didn't harm him." Prosper revealed.

"What?! But me and Dex haven't even been together that long and we always used protection. How did this happen?" A flabbergasted Rae began to cry.

Fragments of the night before slowly revealed themselves to her and she smiled through her tears as she recalled the amazing sex that Prosper told her they'd had. He wasn't lying about it being the best. Then she recalled calling

Dex and hearing Zo in the background having sex. She was having a baby with a down low brother. What a day!

Suddenly something that Prosper had said stuck out to her.

"Did you say harm *him*? I'm less than two months along, how in the hell can they tell than I'm having a boy so soon?!" Rae pondered.

She knew that genetic testing could detect the sex of a baby/embryos immediately, however, that was not typically performed during emergency room visits.

"I see nothing gets past your sexy ass. You aren't having that nigga's baby, Desirae. You are four months pregnant with my son! Prosper beamed to a shocked Rae.

## « Chapter 29 I Worry About My Worries »

"YO P, I'M ABOUT TO head out and meet this baddie that I've been talking to for a little minute online. She is bad as fuck, cousin. She could be Janelle Monáe's little thick sister! Definitely wifey material." Charlie announced.

"Nigga please! Shorty is probably catfishing! You are gonna pull up to a big bitch named Beulah." Prosper clowned.

"Shiiiiiddddd! You got me messed up. You know I've already FaceTimed ole' girl. I may have been born at night, but it wasn't last night, fool. For niggas to be catfished in this day and age is absolutely ludicrous!" Charlie slurred in his Mike Tyson voice.

They both shared a laugh before Prosper said, "Fool get

your ass on somewhere. Don't forget to strap up this time too.

I'm not letting your dirty dick ass use my health insurance card anymore. You know Claryssa almost killed my ass when she logged in and saw that I had an STI via MyChart. Remember, use my card for honorable diseases only!"

"Yeah, yeah, yeah! I remember." Charlie replied dismissively heading out the door.

That was a week ago, and no one had heard or seen Charlie since. Charlie's mom was the manager of his restaurant and she immediately knew something was horribly wrong when he failed to report to his business two consecutive days in a row. Charlie's mom, her twin Shawn, and Prosper hit the pavement themselves. They all had keys to his home and what they found there put even more fear and dread in their hearts.

Charlie's house was ransacked. Charlie was by no means a neat freak, but he would've never kept his home in that condition. His phone and wallet were however missing. Since Charlie was an adult, black and male, the cops refused to file a missing persons' report. They felt that he was young and had the means to vacation and disappear voluntarily whenever he felt the urge to do so.

They nonchalantly shrugged their lazy shoulders and gave them the generic "he'll turn up" speech. Charlie's family knew that he'd never just voluntarily disappear like that. He would've told them where he was going. He could be impulsive, but not in situations like that. He never went out of town or vacationed without Prosper anyway.

The family made fliers and posted them all over the city. It wasn't until Prosper contacted the news and radios stations that the police decided to finally file a missing persons case for Charlie. A hundred thousand dollars was being offered for his safe return. In the beginning, the family was hopeful that he was just being held captive for ransom money, however, the demand call he had hoped for never came.

With each passing day without Charlie, he knew that his cousin's chances of still being alive were growing slimmer and slimmer. Prosper had long shared with the police that his cousin was headed on a date with a female that he'd met online prior to disappearing. They promised to follow up and comb through his messages through his social media and dating apps. Prosper and Charlie's mom were able to give the police the passcodes that he most often used.

Prosper personally logged into the dating app that he knew that his cousin frequented, but the picture of the Janelle look alike had vanished. Her entire account had been deleted. Not easily deterred he accessed his cousin's iCloud and breathed a sigh of relief when he noticed that Charlie had screenshotted the girl's picture.

He eagerly forwarded the picture of her to the detective covering his cousin's case and before long, her picture was all over the news and social media sites. She was presumably the last person to see Charlie and that bitch had some explaining to do.

Charlie said that he had FaceTimed her, so the bitch truly did exist out there somewhere. She was so attractive and exotic looking that someone had to know her. She wasn't someone who could easily glide by unnoticed. The waiting was brutal and Prosper worried about his worries.

He'd often heard people say that having a missing loved one was even more devastating than having a dead one because at least you knew where they were and hopefully had closure.

He now realized that they weren't wrong. Not knowing if Charlie was being tortured, raped, or starved was killing him.

"Yo, talk to me." Prosper said in a hopeful manner.

"Hello, Mr. Collins. How are you today?" Detective Sills inquired.

"Well that all depends on what you're calling to tell me." Prosper replied.

"We followed up on a lead and found out that the woman we've been looking for is named Pilar Tarver. Unfortunately, upon entering Tarver's home, the officers heard a single gunshot coming from one of the bedrooms. They called out and there was no response. Long story short, her body was discovered shortly thereafter. She'd died from a single self-inflicted gunshot wound to the head."

"Damn!!! Now, I know you've got to be gone Charlie! Innocent people just don't go around blowing their fucking brains out for no reason. Fuck! Fuck! Fuck!!!" Prosper began to spaz inconsolably.

He no longer heard anything that the detective was saying to him. He just wanted his best friend back. Claryssa took the phone from her husband and talked to the detective for a brief moment before hanging up and embracing her distraught man. There was nothing that she could say that would ease his pain, however, she prayed that her physical presence reminded him that she too was his best friend and that he wasn't alone.

Although Charlie's mom was technically his next of kin, she depended on Prosper to handle all the dealings of her son's case. She just couldn't bear it. She knew that her only nephew had more strength in his pinky than she possessed in her entire body. News of Tarver's suicide shook their community.

Although Charlie was not a celebrity nationally, he was well known and loved by everyone who came in contact with him.

Charlie was so selfless and never forgot about his humble beginnings. He fed pretty much anybody that came into his restaurant whether they had money or not. At the end of the night instead of pitching left over food, he would personally deliver the leftovers to the massive homeless community downtown.

Cadaver dogs were brought over to Pilar's house and wasted no time fixating on the suspicious patch of disturbed dirt in her two-acre backyard. Sadly, for all of those who loved Charlie, the unearthing of his violent demise was being broadcasted live for the world to see, including Prosper.

Prosper's reaction to Charlie's death was so traumatizing that through her own grief, his aunt had to pick up a small vase and knock him out cold. She then called for an ambulance, because she knew that psychiatric assistance was the only way that Prosper would make it out of the tragedy alive.

# « Chapter 30 Bulletproof »

"HE TOLD ME HE was bulletproof! He told me he was bulletproof! Bulletproof! Bulletproof! Bullet...Proooooooofffffff!!!" A restrained Prosper yelled.

"Let me go!!! I'm going to kill those muthafuckas. I need to kill them! Give me a gun so that I can kill them!" He continued.

"Can you please just give him something already?! I can't stand to see him like this anymore!" Charlie's mom yelled at the nurse who then took off out of the room.

Prosper's family bawled as they watched Prosper have a mental breakdown. He was still in the emergency room because the psychiatric unit had no available beds. Claryssa was at home with both Serena and BJ and everyone was grateful for that because a distraught Rae burst into the room and rushed right up to Prosper's bedside. She hadn't even noticed the other people in the room.

His hands were restrained on either side of him, so she spread her arms so that she could place each of his hands into hers. She then climbed into the bed and leaned forward to kiss away his tears. Seeing him calm down a little, she laid her head over his chest and listened to his heart for a few moments before humming a song that she'd written years ago about him.

Just as the nurse returned with a shot mixed with a benzo and an antipsychotic, soft snores were heard coming from the pair.

When Prosper woke up, he initially forgot all about what had happened to Charlie, but was soon reminded when he spotted his family sprawled out all over his hospital room. A small smile graced his face when he noticed a pregnant Desirae lying next to him instead of his wife. At least now the awkward introductions were out of the way. He was no longer homicidal, just incredibly sad. He couldn't even imagine living in a world that didn't include his cousin. Shit was crazy.

After talking to the psychiatrist, he assured him that he was not a danger to himself or anyone else. He wasn't sure if the doctor fully believed him or if he just wanted to free up the bed that he had been occupying, but at any rate, Prosper was free to go home the same day.

Or at least a home. Since he took an ambulance to the hospital, he simply rode to Rae's house with her. She made sure to pull into her garage so that no one would spot Prosper walking into her front door. Rae took off from work and did her best to repair her love's internal wounds.

She allowed him to cry on her shoulder. She fed and bathed him when he was too weak to. She even sucked him off with no questions asked, if his dick stood at attention too long. She did her best to anticipate his every need so that he wouldn't even have to ask.

By day four, he woke up and suddenly he felt different. He was still sad, but realized that Charlie would want him to continue on without him. Finally cutting his phone on, it took over five minutes before the notifications stopped pouring in. He didn't bother listening to any messages or reading any texts.

His first call was to his mother.

"Hello, hello ma?" He whispered into the phone.

"Prosper, where the hell have you been?! You had us worried sick! Your wife has been going crazy not knowing where you've been. BJ is just..." His mother started before he cut her off.

The mere mention of BJ made his eyes water as he regretted his selfish disappearance. He felt horrible for his inconsiderate actions, but he truly did not see how he would be a help to anyone in the frame of mind he had been in recently.

"I'm so sorry. I have just been having a really hard time with this right now. My heart feels as if it's been ripped from my chest. What am I supposed to do now?" He asked fighting back tears.

Tears freely flowed down Rae's cheeks as she watched the broken man before her. She couldn't think of anything that she could say or do to ease his pain.

"Well, if you would have answered your God damn phone, you would've known that the body that was found, is not Charlie!" Shawn shrieked full of hope.

"Hunh? What do you mean the body isn't Charlie?" He questioned in a confused manner.

"Well, I don't know how much you remember from the day that the body was found, but the body that was unearthed was severely burned. So much so that it was unrecognizable. We were hoping that you could go down to the medical examiner's office to identify the body, but we couldn't reach you. So, when we finally worked up the nerve to go ourselves, we were informed that the body could only be identified via dental records.

Truthfully, we thought they were just wasting their time since we knew it couldn't be anyone but Charlie. Imagine our surprise when we were notified that the dental records matched some poor guy named Fierce Greyson. While I feel horrible for his family, I am so excited for ours. We still don't know where that knucklehead is, but he is still out there and he is alive, baby!"

Prosper literally had to pinch himself to match sure that he wasn't dreaming. He looked up to the heavens and silently thanked God. Although Charlie could still be in grave danger, the sliver of hope that they now had pumped the much needed life back into his body. He suddenly had never felt more rested. Still listening to his mother ramble on, he quickly dressed and ran out of Rae's house without so much as a 'kiss my ass'.

## « Chapter 31 Closed Curtains »

"**I DON'T KNOW WHAT'S** going on with you, Rae, but I don't like it. Why have you been giving me the silent treatment? If I have done something to upset you, I really wish that you would woman up and speak on the shit!" An angry Zo shouted to an unbothered Rae.

Continuing to concentrate on her fully stocked pantry, she had more pressing decisions to make such as whether she wanted the red-hot flaming hot Cheetos or if she wanted the jalapeño flavored ones. Her baby was craving something crunchy and spicy, yet she just couldn't decide on the degree of spicy in which she should choose from.

Zo's fake ass was interrupting her peace and his whining was Harlem Shaking on her last nerve. She had nothing to say to him and she assumed that her silence made that crystal clear.

For the life of her Rae just couldn't understand how Zo could stand in front of her with absolutely no remorse over his actions. His callousness absolutely terrified her. She wondered if she ever really knew him at all. Zo had been her day one since as long as she could remember, but now she wasn't sure where their friendship stood.

Rae could care less about Dex per se, but it was just the principle of it all to her. Why would Zo hook her with Dex if he was even remotely attracted to him? Dex was nice enough, a good distraction from Prosper when she needed him. However, she didn't see him in her long-term future or anything.

Zo had crossed a line that shouldn't have ever been crossed. He was like family but was willing to throw it all away for some dick. The very thoughts of it all made her slam the door to her pantry and make a beeline to her master bedroom. Quickly locking the door behind her, she barely reached the bathroom door when yellow stomach acid spewed all over her bathroom tile, splashing up onto her feet.

In between heaves she managed to make it over her toilet bowl which made her retch even more. Something about throwing up into a toilet never sat right with her. After puking her guts out for the better part of ten minutes, she was exhausted, sore and empty. Very empty. Her pregnancy bladder always failed her when she vomited. Glancing around her bathroom she couldn't help, but to laugh which soon followed by loud sobs.

She was super emotional even with very insignificant triggers. Surely the mess that she had just created wasn't the reason behind her meltdown was it? She cried the entire time that she cleaned.

Once she finished, she finished she glanced in the mirror and laughed, "Bitch, we don't do bipolar disorders this way! Cut it out." She coaxed, hoping to calm herself down.

After showering and getting herself together, she was happy when she noticed that Zo had left. She really didn't have the energy for him. She just wanted to lounge around and cuddle with Prosper who she hadn't seen since he had darted from her house days ago. She missed him terribly, yet she understood that he had to find his cousin. She'd never want to stand in the way of that. The brief glimpse of grief that she'd witnessed him have was something that she never wanted to see again.

She just hoped that it wouldn't be too much longer before her man came back to her and their unborn baby.

I don't know how much more of this shit I can take. Charlie thought to himself. He was in excruciating pain and was simply living one breathe at a time. He existed somewhere between wakefulness and a coma. He was well aware that his injuries were quite serious, yet he didn't know the true extent of them.

He knew that he did not have long left and prayed for a miracle to help save him. On the fateful day that he had disappeared, he was on his way to meet the beautiful Janelle look-alike, however he never made it to his destination.

While he was driving down an eerily deserted road, one of his tires blew out and he lost control of his vehicle. Despite all of his efforts to regain control of his speeding car, he found himself rolling down a steep wooded area and into a cluster of trees.

He immediately lost consciousness, but he was unsure of how long exactly. He vaguely remembered waking up and it sometimes being light out while others, it was pitch black. As the days went on, he found himself able to stay awake a little longer each time. Luckily, he was a semi junkie person, because he did have a small case of water and some snacks and candy in his car to help sustain him. His body was in so much pain that he knew that he had some broken bones, but he was unable to pinpoint which ones they were.

His phone was nowhere to be found and he was trapped as he couldn't get the driver's side door to open. He didn't think that he had the strength to make it to the passenger's side door, but he knew that he had to at least try. He knew many days had passed and he still hadn't been rescued yet. He was losing hope of ever being found so he knew that he had to at least try to help himself.

Bracing himself for the pain, Charlie released a loud animalistic yell as he flung his upper body across the front of his mangled vehicle. As the pain seemingly sprouted throughout his body as if he was being electrocuted, he cried grown man tears. Almost ready to throw in the towel, flashes of his family raced into his mind. He couldn't go out like that. He was a survivor and there was nothing that he couldn't overcome.

Releasing another loud roar, he leapt and reached the other side. Pushing the heavy door open, he used his upper body strength to pull his body out of the car. His legs trailed behind him at odd angles. He was afraid to even look at them. After tossing himself from the car, his was exhausted. His respirations were rapid, and the pain paralyzed him.

"I need a quick nap before I can go any further." He whispered to himself as his heavy eyes closed their curtains.

## « Chapter 32 100 Bands »

"AYE YALL, I APPRECIATE you for meeting with me. I appreciate the cop's efforts, but I still feel like they're not trying as hard as they would if my cousin were a white man. I had a dream and I know that my cousin is still alive, but I know if he is not found like, today, then he won't be for long.

Now in my dream, I saw my cousin in some woods. I don't know if he fell asleep at the wheel try to avoid hitting something, but my cousin is trapped in his car and in the woods and I don't know where. But I suspect that he is somewhere from his house to that bitches house."

Glancing around at the crowd of people who loved his cousin, he smiled when he noticed Sam, Ant, and Rae join them. Rae was absolutely glowing and only he knew why. Their eyes met for a quick moment before he noticed Ant mean mug him followed by Sam gently elbowing Rae.

Clearing his throat, he said, "Thanks to some people who owed me a few favors in the police department, I was able to borrow four canines. Their trainers will be here and assisting us through this search. Two will be specifically attempting to track Charlie's scent, while the other two are specialized cadaver dogs.

Now there is a twelve-mile distance from Charlie's house to Pilar's so we will split up into two groups. One group will start at the woods closest to Charlie's house while the other group will start near Pilar's house. We know that he was headed North towards her house, so try to focus more on that side of the road, if possible. Everyone has been given packets they contain a recent picture of him and his loud ass yellow car. His flashy ass shouldn't be too hard to miss." He joked getting slightly emotional.

He missed his crazy ass cousin severely.

As the group chuckled knowingly regarding Charlie, Prosper pulled it together, divided up the groups and they got to it. The group that started near Charlie's house had eleven volunteers and two dogs while his group had ten people and two dogs. Driving near Pilar's house filled him with dread. Since her house was surrounded by woods, they literally parked on her property and started their search on foot.

They followed the dogs lead as they all kept their eyes open for skid marks and Charlie's vehicle. He silently prayed with each disappointed step he took and no Charlie. He just had to find him today. They were only granted unauthorized use of the dogs for that one day. He promised his mom and his aunt that he would bring Charlie back home...alive. He couldn't let them down. His little sister and his daughter's weren't the same either. They loved their favorite cousin as much as he did.

The Texas heat was set on hell as perspiration poured from their bodies, yet no one complained. Everyone was transfixed on the task at hand. There was still a reward out for whoever found his cousin and he still planned on honoring it.

Naturally, he had put Rae and his brothers in his group. He didn't agree with Rae joining them initially, however, he enjoyed being in her presence even if they couldn't converse without receiving dirty looks from her brothers.

Rae still wasn't showing and the few times she walked in front of him, he admired the form fitting red booty shorts that clung to her juicy ass. She wore a white backless shirt and white sandals. Her look was simple but crazy sexy. Her curls were pinned up high away from her face and neck.

A few times he tried to rationalize whether or not anyone would notice if he took her into the woods for a quick kitty beating. Shaking his perverse thoughts from his sweaty head, he scolded himself. He wasn't out there for a quickie. From then on, he made his business to not even glance in Rae's direction. She was a distraction.

Using a walkie talkie, he called out to the other group to check on their progress. They informed him that they'd found nothing suspicious and were approaching their fifth mile.

"Shit!" Prosper exclaimed lowly.

His group was already in their fifth mile and with less than a mile left, there were still no signs of Charlie.

"Oh my God! Look! What's that?!" Rae shrieked as she noticed the skid marks that the dogs were barking ferociously near. The canines were practically dragging their trainer down a nearby steep hill. Prosper was literally holding his breath as he approached the top of the hill so that he could peer down.

"Shit! He's down there. Charlie's down there! Someone call for an ambulance!!! Charlie, we are coming, hold on!" Prosper called out.

While it felt like an eternity before he'll arrived, in reality, it was less than ten minutes. The most difficult part was getting EMS down the hill safely to assist Charlie. By that time, his mom and aunt who led the other group had reached them. The two women cried and thanked God when a paramedic yelled up stating that he was still alive, but his pulse was extremely weak and thready. None of that extra shit mattered to them because he was still alive.

Once Charlie was brought up the hill and placed safely into the back of the ambulance, Dawn hopped in and rode with her only child.

Shawn and Prosper hugged all of the volunteers, the trainers and the dogs. He then reached into the bag that he'd been carrying and attempted to divide the reward money equally amongst everyone who had showed up and showed out for his cousin. One by one, everyone turned down the money. Their selflessness further tugged at his heartstrings and he soon found himself crying and sniveling the entire ride back to their respective cars.

# « Chapter 33 Surprise! »

"**Awww! Look at my** nephew!!!" Rae gushed in awe of the newest addition to their growing family.

"He is so freaking handsome, Afrika! Great job mama!" Rae said leaning down to hug her friend who was sitting up in the hospital bed.

"Hey, what about me? I put in the most work sis, If you know what I mean." Sam's goody ass stated humping the air.

Valentina promptly smacked her crazy son in the back of his head causing everyone in the hospital room to fall out into a fit of laughter.

"Stop talking like that in front of my grandson boy." She scolded while her eyes lit up as she stared at baby Yarmel.

"Ma, that little nigga doesn't understand what I'm talking about anyway." He huffed like a child.

Valentina didn't respond to her son, however, she shot him a warning glare. Out of all of her children, he tested her patience the most. You would've thought that he was the youngest of her three children.

"I'm sorry everyone, I got here as soon as I could. My principal couldn't find anyone on such short notice to take over my class and she was already covering for the 10th grade English teacher today." A winded Zo came barging in apologetically.

"Oh no need to apologize Zo, I'm just happy that you made it. Meet your nephew, Yarmel." Afrika said sweetly to Zo.

"Hey, you can set those gifts over here." Sam said to Zo.

"O.M.G, he is gorgeous!!! Look at him. Hi, little guy! I'm your uncle Zo and it is so nice to meet you." Zo crooned causing Yarmel to slowly open his eyes revealing his hazel orbs.

"Oh, my goodness and you have your auntie Rae's eye color. You are going to be knocking hella headboards into walls nephew!" Zo joked catching a slap to the back of his head just like Sam had minutes earlier.

Sam laughed so hard that his ribs ached.

"All of you are gonna learn not to talk that way away him sooner or later!" Valentina scolded, however, she was so proud as she glanced around the room at her loved ones.

She considered them all to be her children...blood or not. They had all turned out wonderfully. She was hard on them and she had high expectations for all of them, but so far, they all superseded them.

Rae still hadn't told anyone that she was expecting yet she knew that she would have to soon, because it was becoming increasingly difficult to hide her now growing belly. The tension between her and Zo had boiled over to the point that he had moved out.

She eventually told him that she knew about him and Dex, because she grew weary of him asking what the cold shoulder was about. He never tried to deny it, but instead immediately started bawling like a baby. He begged for forgiveness over and over again, however, Rae wasn't offering any. At least not at that time. She needed time to evaluate things, them, hell, herself even.

She had trusted Zo with everything, including her life, but now she was wondering if he could be trusted with anything. She thought that her boyfriends were safe around those who she considered family. While she could care less about Dex, Zo knew better. Dex owed her nothing, but Zo did. Still trying to be a decent human being, she never told anyone about what Zo did to her. She didn't want the others to shun him as well.

As she stood mere feet away from him, her anger started to boil over her. Then he had the audacity to bring up her eye color and give her an indirect compliment...screw him! Everyone noticed the tension between the former besties and knew that he had moved out, they just didn't understand why.

While her professional life was booming, her personal life needed to be resuscitated. After Charlie was located, she had seen very little of Prosper. He'd left a generic note taped on her front door stating that what they had done was a mistake and that he needed to try to work things out with his wife.

Turns out that Claryssa was pregnant too. Prosper promised to take care of him financially and physically as much as he could. Being a man of his word, Prosper wired her a hefty amount every week and their baby hadn't even been born yet.

When she first read the note that Prosper had left on her door, she had given him two weeks of purse hell. She keyed his cars, slashed tires, pretended to be a potential client only up leave him hanging and crank called both him and Claryssa at all times of the day and night.

She went full-fledged psychotic. Then one day she woke up and realized that she was better than those childish games. If he wanted to be with his wife, that was his God given right. She was the dummy that was in the wrong.

Of course, Prosper knew it was Rae causing all the drama and chaos, but he knew he deserved it. As he watched the videos of her creeping from her house to his, he couldn't help but chuckle at her boldness. She didn't disgust her identity or anything. He could've parked his vehicles in the garage, but instead opted to allow her to vent her frustrations out through his cars. After all, paint and tires were replaceable.

He felt terrible for leading her on. He was actually prepared to leave Claryssa for Rae and had even gone as far as to ask for a separation. He really wanted to be with Rae, however, when he presented the prospect of separating to his wife, she announced that she was pregnant, and guilt tripped him into staying.

It was difficult wanting to leave Claryssa with one of his kids, surely, he couldn't leave her to care for two. PJ was already a handful. As bad as it hurt, he decided to stay. Not being able to hold Rae and rub her belly and feet felt like torture. He still watched her from his windows, more now than ever.

Charlie was recovering well and mentally was back to

his old self. He had a lot of rehab ahead of him. Both of his femurs were broken and so were most of his ribs. The doctors predicted that if he had been out there for another four hours, our happy ending would've been quite different.

Charlie was shocked upon finding out that Pilar had killed herself and that a badly burned body was found buried on her property. The shit was strange as fuck and the investigation into that entire ordeal was still being investigated.

Charlie spent two long weeks in the hospital prior to being discharged. While the hospital recommended that he be discharged to a rehabilitation facility in order to maximize his therapy, he declined and offered to attend outpatient instead. He was ready to get back to his business.

A surprise party was planned for the day after Charlie was discharged. He was going to be staying with Prosper and Claryssa since he had so many activity restrictions. Claryssa was in charge of the invitations so naturally she invited the brown beauty next door.

Rae was shocked when she received the invite. She questioned whether or not she should actually show up. Once her brothers confirmed that they were also invited and attending, Rae decided to show up. After all, Charlie had always been nice to her unlike his bitch ass cousin.

Naturally, the party was being held at Charlie's restaurant. His employees had prepared all of his favorites in vast amounts. The decorations were on point too. Black and yellow was the theme as his ass loved those colors. The people who were invited showed up an hour earlier than Charlie was expected to. They all mingled and had some drinks in preparation for the man of the hour.

Rae sat with her brothers and Afrika. Valentina had volunteered to baby sit Yarmel. Afrika was still self-conscious about the remaining baby weight that she had, but sis was snatched! That baby had done her figure some justice. She was curvy before, but now, she looked as if she had had a BBL.

Rae had finally told Afrika that she was pregnant by Prosper, however, she just couldn't tell her family that she'd allowed herself to get knocked up by a married man. A married man who unsurprisingly didn't want her and had decided to work things out with his family.

She was such a naive fool. Men rarely left their families for their side pieces, why did she feel that she'd be any different? Wallowing in self-pity in a room of joyous people, Rae was pulled from her thoughts when someone yelled that Charlie was being wheeled in.

Everyone took their positions and waited for the grand finale. As the door swung open, time seemed to freeze as Prosper, Charlie and Claryssa appeared all dressed to the nines. Their mothers trailed in behind them too along with Serena and PJ.

Out of nowhere a seemingly always poised and reserved Ant growled through gritted teeth, "What the fuck?!"

While many people didn't seem to notice, and those who did quickly returned their focus back towards Charlie, Rae, Sam and Afrika grilled Ant. They wanted to know what literally had smoke seeping from his ears. Without another word or even speaking to Charlie, Ant angrily stormed out of the building. Charlie and Prosper tried to speak to him on his way out, but both were left dumbfounded by his cool demeanor.

Glancing at Sam and Rae for answers, they received none as they were greeted with nonchalant shrugs.

"Fuck, that nigga was our ride!" Sam groaned in annoyance.

## « Chapter 34 Puppeteer »

AFTER ANT LEFT, EVERYONE made the best of the party. Prosper was surprised to see that Rae had come. It was nice to see her, and his gaze kept wandering to her midsection. She was definitely showing now. How was she fooling everyone around her still? She tried to hide her belly behind a loose-fitting shirt that flared a little at the base, but the curly haired beauty was definitely showing his son's existence.

He beamed proudly, filled with pride. He loved having a girl, PJ was a certified daddy's girl, but knowing that he had a mini-him on the way just made him love her that much more. Rae's hungry ass decided to raid the food after she hugged and greeted Charlie. Her son loved fried chicken and Mac and cheese already. She couldn't blame him though because the shit was banging.

Afrika and Sam's freaky asses had snuck somewhere. Afrika couldn't have sex, yet since she had just had a baby, but

I'm sure you all can imagine what other possibilities remained for the young, carefree couple. As Rae shoveled forkfuls of her food into her mouth, sheer disappointment spread across her pretty face as she realized that her plate was running low on Mac and cheese. The food line stayed long, and she didn't want to have to wait and risk her other food getting cold in the process.

Just as she'd made up her mind to make her second food run, a heaping fresh plate was placed in front of her. Without glancing up, she mumbled a quick word of gratitude and dove in. It wasn't until he chuckled, and his cologne infiltrated her nostrils that she realized who the Good Samaritan was. Her eating slowed as she self-consciously glanced up at *him*. Uhhh!!! Why did he have to look and smell like that!!! She screamed inwardly.

Sitting next to her uninvited, Prosper whispered, "I miss the fuck out of you Desirae. This is the hardest shit I've ever had to go through...excluding this Charlie shit, of course." He admitted in a whispered tone.

Claryssa was very popular back in high school, so she found herself preoccupied with showboating and comparing her successes to old classmates. She lived for moments like that.

As much his very presence caused her pearl to tingle, she fought her emotions and remained unmoved by his words.

"Good for you Prosper. Why are you over here at my booth? Go and be with your family. Leave me the fuck alone. Me and my son do not need you. You're not even the father so stop sending me money. Kick rocks!" Rae spewed venomously.

Prosper glared silently for a few moments asking God for the strength not to spazz on her silly ass in there. Desirae had better thank her lucky stars that he didn't want to ruin Charlie's party by showing his natural black ass in there.

After calming down, he told himself that she was upset and that he deserved all the abuse that she was dishing out. He was a man, he had tough skin, but the shit that she had said stung. He knew that she was lying through her perfectly white teeth, but he still wasn't feeling the shit. He never wanted to hear the shit again.

Roughly, snatching her legs towards him, he decided to play unfair. Their booth was angled perfectly and obstructed anyone's view of his hands attack under the table. Her skirt was lifted up and her panties were pulled to the side. He wasted no time showing Rae that he truly did miss her and that he was sorry. With each orgasm that rippled through her body, he took the time to lick his fingers dry from her wetness.

He silently tortured her and placed her back under his spell. He had her apologizing for the way that she had spoke to him and promised never to say it again. He almost felt like a puppeteer by the way that he was able to control her with his fingers.

"Fuck this shit." He said willing to risk it all.

Licking his lips at the sight of Rae's erect nipples beneath the thin material of her shirt had him looking for a secluded area for the two of them to reunite.

He glanced at her and she smirked knowingly in approval. As he attempted to readjust his own erection, a guilty looking Afrika and Sam reemerged looking sweaty and disheveled. The slight hint of sex lingered around the two of them...or was it Rae and Prosper's indiscretions? One couldn't be too sure.

Afrika and Sam small talked about nothing significant until Claryssa's loud ass approached the booth. She smiled widely at Rae and took in how gorgeous she looked without even trying much. She hadn't even bothered to beat her face, yet she was stunning. Glowing even. She really did like the woman, especially for helping her out with PJ when her husband was in a coma. She was forever indebted to her.

"Heeyyyy Desirae! I'm so glad you came! Come here and get me some love guuurrrlll!" Claryssa slurred.

Was that bitch drunk!? Rae thought to herself, but didn't mention it out loud. Rae stood up and hugged Claryssa like she had asked, and she definitely smelled alcohol on the expectant woman's breath. Before she could pull completely away from her Claryssa loudly said, "Woah! I see I'm not the only one with a bun in the oven!"

She then proceeded to lift up Rae's shirt and she commenced to rubbing the mortified woman's protruding belly. When Rae summoned up enough courage to look at her brother, he had rage in his eyes, and they were looking directly at a guilty looking Prosper.

# « Chapter 35 Boss Bitch »

"Ewww, what the hell have you all been feeding these little bastards...lead paint?!" Sam chortled in disgust as the family toured the seventh daycare facility in their area that day.

Everyone just shook their heads because he wasn't wrong this time. He had asked a little boy who had to be at least four his name and how old he was, and the boy only knew his nickname and held up two fingers in response to his age.

It had great ratings, but nothing seemed to be good enough for his now eight-week-old son. Sam had already returned to work, yet Afrika couldn't return until reliable childcare was found. In the end, they opted to have a nanny take care of the baby at Afrika's shop while she worked. The bottom line was, Sam wasn't leaving Yarmel anywhere.

Rae knew that her brother was over the top with a lot of things, however, she didn't know if she could leave her son with strangers with when the time came. She was seven months pregnant and feeling it. After a drunken Claryssa outed her pregnancy, Sam wasted no time exposing her to Ant and their parents. Rae had never felt so fearful and so humiliated.

Her saucy mother was so disappointed that she didn't even cuss her foolish daughter out. Valentina had truly hoped that Rae had learned from her previous mistake and had moved on like she promised she would. Sensing that there was no point in beating a dead horse, she decided that her second grandchild would be arriving soon, so she turned lemons into lemonade.

While she acknowledged Rae's pregnancy, she never brought up Prosper and his involvement. She figured it didn't matter because her daughter and grandson would flourish with or without him. She always had before, and a baby wasn't about to change that.

Rae was attending her weekly Lamaze class with Prosper by her side. While he was still with his wife, he had really stepped up. He never missed a doctor's appointment or a Lamaze class. He actually enjoyed the Lamaze classes more than Rae because he was able to publicly molest her without anyone batting an eyelash.

Rae hated that she was so weak for the man who had captured her heart so many years ago. She knew that she deserved more than a few stolen moments from him. She was a boss bitch and any man would be glad to wife her up, yet there she was contentedly completing deep breathing exercises and playing second fiddle. She was someone's deep and dirty little secret and soon her son would join her.

What they had, technically had no title so she knew that

she didn't owe Prosper shit. Even with her growing belly she still managed to turn heads everywhere she went. It was while she was walking out of Afrika's shop that she ran into a cute guy named Chemmo. She'd just had her hair straightened and her brows touched up when ruggedly handsome guy approached her.

She could immediately tell that he was very different from any guy that she had ever come across and she wasn't altogether sure if that was a good or a bad thing. He was from Boston and she found his accent to be very sexy. Like her, he was black and Dominican, but like her brothers, he appeared Puerto Rican. When Chemmo had asked Rae's number, she rolled her eyes and pointed at her rounded belly.

He smiled showcasing beautiful teeth, which Rae silently admired.

He then said, "Okay, so you let some lame knock you up. What does that have to do with me, ma? It must not be too serious because I don't see so much as a promise ring on your fingers or around your neck."

Rae blushed because he had read her and didn't even know her.

Sensing that he'd embarrassed her, he countered, "No need to blush around me. I'm the type of nigga that will put Preparation-H on your hemorrhoids after you deliver your baby. Never feel ashamed around me.

As long as you're transparent with me, I'll be the same with you."

Rae didn't even know how to respond to Chemmo and it was rare that people left her speechless. He was cute and there was a pure sincerity in his tone. She allowed her hazel eyes to fully take him in. He looked like money without being extra flashy. His hair was cut very short. He wasn't all that tall, but he was buff. He definitely devoted a lot of time at the gym. He had dark brown piercing eyes with naturally arched brows. A long scar ran across his otherwise smooth right jaw. It made him look hard and sexy.

Rae felt as if he had placed her in a trance because he had certainly piqued her interests. No other guy besides Prosper had her intrigued that way.

Chemmo was definitely feeling the exotic pregnant beauty. At first, he started to keep it moving once he noticed her swollen stomach, but there was just simply something about her that had him ready to settle down. He was twenty-five and wasn't getting any younger. He had bedded pretty much every type of chick that he cared to. As good as it was, he woke up one day wanting more. Something was pulling him to Desirae, and he wasn't quite sure what it was.

"I know you hear this all day, every day, but you truly are gorgeous." He said to a blushing Rae as he leaned done and placed a soft kiss on her forehead.

Normally she would've flipped out at the mere thought of a stranger placing their lips anywhere near her, but something about those forehead kisses drove her insane. She loved them! After they conversed for a while, they exchanged numbers and had been talking ever since. With Chemmo living in Boston, the phone was their lifeline. There was never a time that she FaceTimed him and he didn't answer even if he simply said that he needed to call her back.

He was so attentive and made her feel like a queen. He was single, had no children and was fine. She was well aware that he was into illegal activities, but that was all he allowed her to know. He told her that the less she knew about, the better.

With her romance with Chemmo starting to blossom, Rae slowly began to distance herself from Prosper.

She was done devoting her time and energy to a dead end. Despite Chemmo's questionable career choice, he was a great guy and she felt that they could truly build something special. After talking for about a month, Chemmo announced that he was coming back to Texas on business. She didn't care what the reason was, she was excited to get to see him again.

## « Chapter 36 Booty Meat »

"HOLY CRAP ZO! WHO in the hell won the fight?!" Afrika squealed waking baby Yarmel up from his nap.

"Damn it!" She growled through gritted teeth.

Laughing Zo replied, "Sis, let's just put it like this, his funky ass managed to block every single punch...with his stupid ass face! I'm tired of these fuck boys forgetting that I have a big ass dick and a pair of balls just like they do. You know I was mad that he actually made me run after him. I'm not chasing nobody's child, hell I have asthma!"

"Lord! Zo, you are so damn crazy! I told you about fooling around with those thugs with the charcoal black lips,

Grey gums and crimson eyes. Leave those undercover niggas alone! But on another note, I've missed the hell out of you! I know things between you and Rae are still rocky, but at the end of the day she still loves you."

"I don't know about that Afrika. She really doesn't want to be my friend anymore. She has me blocked from everything and refuses to talk to me. I know what I did was messed up and by far the biggest mistake of my life. I just want things back the way they used to be!" Zo exclaimed with tears threatening to spill onto his cheeks.

"Things will work out, you'll see. Just as miserable as you are without her, she's equally miserable without you. Trust me. That's why you are going with me to her baby shower today. You two are going to settle this once and for all. Both of you have said that the sex wasn't even all that. I'm not about to have my best friends at each other's throats over some mediocre dick. Now help me get your nephew together, there's still a few more gifts that I'd like to pick up and we need to finish setting things up before the guests arrive." Afrika stated.

"I sure hope you're right about all of this best friend, I sure hope you're right." A nervous Zo whispered to himself.

By the time Afrika and Zo had reached the fourth store, they were both exhausted. They both somehow had to manage arm loads of bags while also pushing Yarmel's stroller.

Before they left, Afrika suggested that they rest on a nearby bench so that she could rest her sore feet for a few minutes.

"Why do you keep glancing around like that silly? You're making me nervous." Afrika chuckled nervously.

"No reason, I just have a weird feeling. Let's just finish up and get the hell out of here." He suggested.

Feeling uneasy by his unease, Afrika stated, "I think we have the entire mall in our arms, let's get out of here."

She hoped that her relaxed demeanor and brave front calmed his nerves a little. As they made their way back towards the front of the mall, Afrika noticed Zo continuing to glance about the place, however not seeming to find what he was looking for.

Once they reached Afrika's minivan, she got Yarmel strapped in in record time. Once the doors were locked and her foot pressed the accelerator, they both silently breathed sighs of relief. She didn't know what the hell was going on, but shit didn't feel right. Zo's paranoid ass was definitely catching an Uber back home. Even Yarmel could feel the negative energy and was wailing loudly in the backseat. Luckily, Rae didn't live too far from the mall.

As Afrika grabbed her tearful child along with some of the bags from the trunk, she realized that Zo hadn't budged.

"Umm hello! Earth to Zo! What is with you today goofy? Come and pretend to be a gentleman and either help me with the bags or your spoiled nephew." She fussed almost regretting bringing her friend.

Glancing at Yarmel he smiled lowly and shook his head. Instead he grabbed all of the bags and trailed behind the two.

∞

*Girl, shake that booty meat*

*That booty meat*

*Shake that booty meat*

*That booty meat*

*Girl shake that booty meat all up on me*

*Soulja Boy up in this thing, come and hang with me*

*I'm your ace boon coon, drink Champagne with me*

*Take a bubble bath, come and switch lanes with me*

*I'm the number one stunna, let me see what you got*

*I'm the baller round town, let me see how you pop*

*I'm your girl best friend lets see how you hawk*

*Put that thing in the air then make it drop*

"What in the ghetto is going on in here!" A shocked Afrika chuckled at the sight of Rae and her early helpers already partying and twerking to Soulja Boy's rachet classic.

Everyone fell into a fit of laughter at Afrika's reaction with the exception of Rae. She wore an angry scowl on her pretty face. Her orbs were fixated on an antsy Zo. He was never afraid of anyone or anything, however there was something about Rae when she was upset. Just as he was about to tell Afrika that him coming was a huge mistake and leaving, Rae slowly waddled her pregnant butt over to him.

Still glaring at him, she drew her right hand back as far as she could get it and slammed it into his right cheek. A stunned Zo immediately brought his hands up to cover his stinging face. As everyone rushed over to prevent her from attacking him again, however she raised her arm instantly freezing everyone where they stood,

She again shocked everyone when she began to sob hysterically before wrapping her arms around the man that she had always considered a third brother. A stunned Zo didn't know how to react. He enjoyed her embraced, but feared that any sudden movement from him would trigger Rae to attack again. After a few more moments passed and she hadn't hit him again, she slowly wrapped his arms around his sister and joined in on the tear fest. Never one to be left out, Afrika walked over and joined her best friends.

# « Chapter 37 Grey Gums »

**"WHAT KIND OF ANIMAL** would've done this to him!!!" Rae wailed loudly with her head resting on Chemmo's chest.

*After the trio all kissed and made up, it was just like old times. As usual Zo's flamboyant charm was the life of the party. Rae was initially furious that Afrika had brought Zo to her baby shower, but after watching him awkwardly squirm under her gaze, it tugged at all of her soft spots that she had for him.*

*Truthfully, she was tired of being angry with him. Hell, without the anger clouding her judgment anymore, she now realized that he had done her a favor. Had the two not have slept together, she might still be wasting her time dating that confused simpleton. She had now moved onto bigger and better things also known as Chemmo.*

*She had a nice turn out and knew that she wouldn't have to buy her son anything until he was at least three years old. She had never felt more loved. Everyone who meant something to her were in attendance, male and female. She didn't discriminate.*

*From the outside looking in, most would've assumed that Chemmo was the doting expectant father. He was so attentive and good to Rae. She was really starting to fall for him. While she knew that she'd always have feelings for Prosper, especially since the child they'd created together was growing inside of her womb, she knew that they would most likely never be.*

*Chemmo was a pleasant distraction. She could definitely see him in her and her son's future. Prosper's sneaking ass would never be permitted to help her raise their child openly. She knew that all he could offer was financial support, however it took more than finances to raise a child.*

*Naturally Prosper was not happy about her seeing someone else, however she was grown, and his married ass had no room to talk. She told him as much too. He'd tried creeping over to her house as he usually did and was thoroughly surprised when he realized that she'd changed her locks on his ass. He felt her slipping away from him and he felt so defeated.*

*He needed to do something and quickly before he lost her forever. He'd be damned if that bastard ever had the opportunity to be around his seed.*

*As usual Prosper was present with Claryssa, however his eyes remained glued on Rae and Chemmo. He was rageful and ready to snap every time he saw that punk touch her.*

*"Bae is everything okay? You've been tense since we got here." A worried Claryssa whispered in Prosper's ear.*

*"What? Yeah, yeah. I'm cool, just a little tired, I guess. I'll be alright."*

"Well if you say so." She shrugged not sure if she bought his story.

"I guess I'm a little tired too so I'm just going to go ahead and let your baby rest." She smiled patting her rounded belly.

"Do you want me to walk you home?" He asked.

"No love, it's just the next yard over. I'm sure that I can manage to find my way." She joked.

Relieved, he shot her a quick, phony smile so that he could direct his attention back on his girl and baby.

"Damn, where the hell did she go that fast?" He mumbled to himself as he stood to his feet.

As he went room to room, he was baffled when he couldn't find her. He had seen Chemmo playing with her brothers, but where was she?

He finally decided to check outside and was surprised to see her in the pool alone. With her back towards him, he quickly stripped down to his boxers and got into the water with her. He knew that he was making an extremely bold move, but he just didn't give a fuck.

Once he reached her, her released his erection from the hole in the front of his boxers. He then pulled the crotch of her yellow one-piece bathing suit to the side. He swiftly entered her drenched box from the back. She felt so good and it had been so long since he had been inside of her, so he knew that he'd be cumming soon.

His eyes closed as he thrusted in and out of her. When he felt her vaginal muscles convulse, he couldn't help, but to release a stifled moan into the nape of her neck as he too exploded in ecstasy. Unbeknownst to them both, someone had stumbled upon their voyeuristic affair.

*Attempting to get her breathing under control, she said,*

*"Prosper, we can't keep doing this. You need to let me go. You are married with a child on the way. Make your marriage work. Just let me go, because he really does make me happy."*

*As a stunned Prosper was about to respond, a rapid session of gunfire was heard coming from the front of the house.*

## « Chapter 38 For Sale »

IT WAS UNCLEAR AS TO whether or not Chemmo would pull through. They relied heavily on their faith to see them through their tragedy. The doctors didn't appear hopeful and their energy was clearly felt. A procedure was done to hopefully alleviate the swelling in his brain. Tests would be performed later by the neurologist to determine if there was any hope.

All Rae could do was cry when Chemmo's family arrived from out of town and instructed her and her visitors to leave. They weren't shy about telling her that she was the reason for his untimely death, and they weren't altogether wrong. According to the witnesses at her baby shower, he had stormed angrily past them and headed straight out of the front door. That is when his was caught off guard and struck three times by an unknown assailant.

Apparently Chemmo had also texted his cousin about catching Rae fucking her baby daddy in the pool at her baby shower. He told his cousin that he was through with hoes and was headed home. If only he knew how prophetic that statement would turn out to be. She was devastated, but also felt that she had no right to be. She along with Zo and Afrika walked solemnly out of the room where a deceased Chemmo laid.

He didn't deserve that shit. Afrika continued watching a nervous Zo. She put her finger on it, but he'd never been so on edge before in his life. He knew without a shadow of a doubt that those bullets were intended for him. Grey gums had mistaken Chemmo for Zo. They were wearing similar colored clothing and were about the same height and complexion. He felt horrible and was terrified to tell Rae out of fear that she'd turn her back on him for good that time.

After wallowing in guilt and turmoil for hours, Zo decided to come to tell his friends about his suspicions. He wasn't one hundred percent and he knew that Chemmo was into illegal activities. Surely, he had an enemy out there somewhere, however Zo knew better. The nigga who he'd fucked and then fucked up was trying to kill him. He needed to be stopped before he realized that he had shot and killed the wrong man.

"Rae...Afrika...I need you both to sit down and listen to what I'm about to tell you. Do not interrupt, let me finish and then you can ask me whatever you want to, okay?"

"Okay," they chimed in unison.

Zo took one long inhalation and soon exhaled the story in its entirety. The two women listened intently. While Rae quietly sobbed, she never once interrupted him as he'd requested. Once his confession concluded, the silence was deafening. His eyes darted from woman to woman as he waited for a reaction. After a few moments, Rae ran up to Zo and hugged him. That display of love and affection left not one dry eye in the room.

"Oh my God, Zo! That could have been you in the morgue! I would have died if something had happened to you. I adored and really cared about Chemmo. I truly hate what happened to him, but I absolutely love you!"

"I love you, too Desirae!" Zo wailed.

Sniffling, Rae said, "I've got to call my brothers to see about ridding us of our little assassin."

It took just a few hours for grey gums to be eliminated. Apparently, he didn't feel the need to hide or protect himself as he didn't view Zo as a threat. What he'd failed to realize was that his besties were his secret weapons. The streets aren't for everyone, that's why they made sidewalks.

They always had his back even through his hiccups. Zo did not ask for any details or specifics because the truth was, he didn't want to know. The mere fact that the bastard was gone, was enough for him to immediately breathe better.

Even Prosper felt bad for the guy competing for Rae's love and affection. No one deserved to be gunned down senselessly like a dog. He could not help but to wonder if his evil thoughts of the man had anything with his untimely death. They say the power of the mind is out of this world. After his evening spent with Rae at their son's baby shower, he was ecstatic when she didn't resist him in the pool.

He couldn't believe his luck when she had actually allowed him access to her body once again, especially out in the open the way they had been. He had finally admitted to himself that he had fallen deeply and madly in love with the hazel eyed beauty. He couldn't lie to himself or his wife anymore.

Seeing her interactions with Chemmo had fucked him up even more so than seeing her with the other little guys that she'd brought around. A real nigga recognized a real nigga and even he could see that Chemmo was a solid guy. Rae looked at him differently. He could see that she genuinely liked him. Dude was a threat.

Chemmo could have smashed Rae and left her pregnant ass alone, but he didn't. Prosper had a feeling that Chemmo would've taken good care of Rae and their unborn child. Unfortunately, it was that selfish part of him that was happy that he no longer had to compete with his ass.

Prosper was at Charlie's soul food spot and had laid it all out in front of his crazy cousin. Charlie had made a full recovery and it was back to business as usual.

"Well cuzzo, for the hundredth time, you know I'm team Meg...I mean team Desirae all day. She is who makes you happy and nigga, seeing you happy, makes me happy. You don't have to be with Claryssa in order to raise your seeds. File for joint cutody. You would easily win. Follow your heart and ya lil dick nigga!" Charlie schooled his older cousin.

Rubbing his face in a frustrated manner, Prosper stated, "Fuck you! They don't call me Big P for nothing!" He joked.

"Naw, but seriously, you are right. I can't keep stringing C along. She deserves better than that. We haven't really even had sex since she got pregnant and to be honest, I'm not even sweating it. I don't even want to honestly. It's so different this time. When she was pregnant with PJ, I was all over her ass, but not this time. All I can think about is Desirae and what a future with her would entail." Prosper stressed.

"Well it sounds like a wise decision has been made. I'm proud of you fool." Charlie stated seriously.

Across town, Rae was in absolute turmoil. Filled with regret and grief, she didn't know if she would ever forgive herself for what happened to Chemmo. Being a firm believer in karma, she had no doubt in her mind that sexing Prosper had led to Chemmo's demise.

He was too good for her anyway. He deserved better than her. She decided to take the summer off from school so that she could focus more on her pregnancy and mental health. While it would surely push her graduation date back a little, Rae knew that it was necessary.

Everyone felt especially horrible for Rae. Not only was her potential new love violently murdered in front of her house, her baby shower was tarnished. She knew that her baby shower would easily go down as the worst baby shower in history. She felt as if everything that she'd received on that day was bad luck and she had no intentions on keeping any of it. It was she who had washed Chemmo's blood from in front of the home that she had loved so much.

Placing a For Sale sign in front of what she once considered her dream home, she knew that there was only one way to completely shed her of her internal demons and frequent nightmares. So much bad had taken place since receiving ownership of her beloved home. She had to get rid of her house and Prosper once and for all.

## « Chapter 39 In...deed »

PROSPER WASN'T REALLY sure what or how to think. He was finally becoming the man that he needed to be for Rae, yet he was a little too late. His timing always seemed to be off. He had finally manned up and requested a divorce from Claryssa and had even moved out. The look of devastation on Claryssa's face damn near made him change his mind, however he knew he'd only be staying for all the wrong reasons.

He wanted to be happy and he wanted the same for his soon to be ex-wife. He felt responsible for the dissolution of their marriage, therefore he was willing to leave her the house and divide everything they'd built together over the years. His only request was equal custody of their children. That matter was nonnegotiable.

Prosper had always considered himself to be an honorable and honest dude. He sat down with Claryssa and laid out all of his cards. He told her that he was in love with someone else and had possibly had always been. He told her that he was expecting a baby with the love of his life and that he no longer wanted to lie to either of them any longer. One thing that he did not disclose, was who the woman was. With Rae living just next door, he knew no good would come from it.

He kicked himself for creating such a messy situation. When he actually sat back and thought about all of his actions leading up to that point, all he could do is shake his head at the brazenness of it all. He actually had the audacity to move the browned beauty, whom he always considered beautiful into the house next to where he lived with his own family. Shit like that was just underheard of.

In his defense, he did try to resist her. Hell, he even pulled different tricks in order to get her to resist him, but it was all in vain. The chemistry between the two of them was electrifying and it was that gravitational pull that let him know that he had to have her.

Prosper could've moved in with his mom and sister or even crashed at Charlie's, however he just wanted to be alone. Well, that wasn't altogether true, he wanted to be with Desirae, but her ass was back on her bullshit. He could not reach her yet again. To make matters even worse, he noticed that her ass was selling her damn house! Who does that while they are pregnant? She was definitely tweaking.

Since her little boyfriend died, Desirae had virtually ghosted him. He knew that she was hurting, but didn't understand why she was shutting him out, especially since he was finally ready for her.

"Man, what would you do if you were me? She won't talk to me." Prosper confided in his cousin.

"Honestly, in order to show her that you are serious this time, you are going to have to come with your A game. It won't be easy, but anything is possible if you want it bad enough. Now listen up..." Charlie once again schooled his lovesick cousin.

Once Charlie finished telling Prosper what he felt he should do, Prosper's jaw hit the ground.

"Nigga what? Man, you can't be serious! I'm not trying to go out like that for real. I'll admit, I love her ass, but I'm not trying to go out like a chump either!" Prosper protested.

"Suit yourself. I'm telling you, if you do that shit then I guarantee you that you'll get your girl. When have I ever steered you in the wrong direction?"

Prosper cut his eyes sharply at his mischievous cousin prompting Charlie to chuckle and throw both hands up defensively.

"Okay, okay, well maybe I've gotten us into a few hiccups here and there, but this is different. Do what you want though." Charlie stated matter-of-factly.

"So, you're sure about this, hunh?" Prosper asked rubbing the fine hairs of his goatee.

"In...deed!" Charlie said raising each of his chest muscles up one at a time to match each syllable of the word.

Prosper just shook his head he knew exactly where Charlie's crazy as had gotten that shit from.

∞

"No...no...wait! Please don't hang up!" Prosper shouted pleadingly into the phone.

Releasing a frustrated raspberry into the phone, Afrika said "What the hell does your married ass want Prosper? You have put my friend through enough. How in the hell did you get my number anyway?"

Ignoring her irritated tone because he needed her, he answered, "I begged and paid Sam a pretty penny for it, "He admitted.

"But please listen. I left my wife. I am ready to step up to the plate and be the man that Desirae needs me to be. I want to be there for her and for our baby. I know we didn't start off the right way, but I promise you if you help me get her back, I'll never hurt her again. You have my word, sis. Help me." Prosper pleaded like Jodeci.

He was met with silence from her, but he knew that she was still on the line because he could hear her baby fussing in the background.

Finally, she spoke up and said, "Just for the record, I'm not doing this shit for you. I'm doing this for my friend and my nephew in her stomach. If you screw me over and hurt them at any point in the future, I will kill you myself...with my bare hands."

Before Prosper could thank Afrika or even let her in on her game plan, she hung up in his face. All he could do was chuckle and shake his head at the mean, petite African woman. He could only admire the love that she felt towards the love of his life. He made a silent vow to himself. If she agreed to be with him, he would spend the rest of his life making her happy.

# « Chapter 40 House Is Not A Home »

"EwwW WHY ARE YOU two acting so weird today?! What's up? Where are y'all taking me now? I told you both that I have a potential buyer coming to meet me at the house in a little while so make this shit quick!" An irritated and impatient Rae snapped at her two best friends.

Afrika and Zo had kidnapped their bestie earlier that morning claiming to want to have a fun-filled day of pampering to cheer her up. Rae appreciated the gesture, however all she wanted to do was lie around her house eating, sleeping, and packing. Since she had been with her friends, virtually every surface of her body had been violated in some way.

She had her nails and toes done. Brows and body waxed. She'd had a full body massage. Her hair had been straightened and face was beautiful with a gorgeous arrangement of makeup. She had also been fitted with a beautiful gown that hugged her voluptuous curves and caressed her large baby bump. She had never felt more beautiful, but now she was growing exhausted and was famished.

Once she noticed that Afrika had pulled up in front of Charlie's soul food restaurant, she eyeballed both of her friends suspiciously. They offered her no explanation and pretended to not to notice her evil glare.

Afrika and Zo got out of the car and did not wait for their friend to protest. They instead began walking towards the large building. Rae sat in the car pouting and with her arms folded across her ample chest for a few minutes before the delicious smells wafting from the restaurant made her stomach growl loudly.

"Damn it. Well fine! I'll come and eat, but then we are leaving!" Rae shouted to herself as she got out.

Pushing the heavy door open she nearly had a heart attack when she heard, "Surprise!"

There were probably one-hundred familiar faces there smiling at her. They had recreated her baby shower and in the center of the room she couldn't help but to notice the man who had stolen her heart when she was just an awkward teenager. He was dressed to the nines and the stirring in her panties had her pinching herself to break free from her trance.

Her parents and brothers came over and embraced her lovingly. They explained everything to her and how Prosper had put everything together for that day. After mingling with all of the guest for about thirty minutes, she smelled him behind her.

Slowly turning around, she resisted the urge to smile at him. He knew her so well. He came equipped with a heaping plate of all of her favorite foods. When she went to reach for it, he swiped her manicured hand a way. Instead, he commenced to feeding her. At first, she found it awkward and was too hungry for his mind games. She wanted to smash her plate. But she decided to play it cool and not embarrass him in front of all of the onlookers.

She decided to accept the bites as he professed his loved to her. He told her how beautiful she was and had even explained to her how he was divorcing Claryssa. Something about the mentioning of her name snapped Rae out of her fairy tale because she immediately pushed him away and went to make her own plate. Sitting down she noted that she still had approximately two hours left before she needed to meet with her potential buyer.

They claimed to want to purchase the house in cash and had even offered her one-hundred thousand more than what she was asking for if she could be moved out within a week. She definitely couldn't allow that deal to slip through her fingers.

Deep in her thoughts, she nearly missed Prosper walking onto the newly added stage.

When he grabbed the microphone, she sank deeper into her seat as she said, "Oh lord," under her breath. She was so into what he was doing that she didn't even notice her family beaming at her.

"Hello everyone, as many of you may already know, my name is Prosper. I'm going to sing a song for yall today. I'm nervous as hell so I want you to bear with me and not make me feel any crazier than I already do. I am dedicating this song to the most beautiful woman that I've ever met." Prosper stated boldly looking at an embarrassed Rae.

"Lord, what is this fool doing? He is about to make an ass out of himself in front of all of these people." She whispered to her bestfriends who just laughed their asses off.

They couldn't wait to hear the fuckery themselves.

When the music started playing, the room went silent and all eyes were glued on Prosper.

*"Doo doo doo doo doo*

*Doo doo doo doo doo doo doo doo doo*

*Doo doo doo doo doo doo doo doo doo doo doo*

*Oh, oh, oh, oh, oh"*

A complete word hadn't been spoken yet the crowd was in shock of the likeness between Prosper and the late great Luther's voice.

*"A chair is still a chair, even when there's no one sittin' there*

*But a chair is not a house and a house is not a home*

*When there's no one there to hold you tight*

*And no one there you can kiss goodnight*

*Whoa, oh, oh, oh, oh, oh, oh*

*Girl*

*A room is a still a room, even when there's nothin' there but gloom*

*But a room is not a house and a house is not a home*

*When the two of us are far apart*

*And one of us has a broken heart*

*Now and then I call your name*

*And suddenly your face appears*

*But it's just a crazy game*

*When it ends, it ends in tears"*

Rae's makeup was ruined as tears streamed down her face uncontrollably. As Prosper continued to sing, he had slowly walked from the stage and was now belting in front of her giving her a private show. Everyone cheered them on and was still in shock that Prosper could actually blow.

Once the song ended, Prosper again shocked everyone when he removed a black box from his pocket and kneeled down on one knee. Rae herself gasped and clutched her imaginary pearls.

As Prosper began to speak, he too became a little choked up as he said, "Desirae Sanchez, you are one of the most important people in my life. I have made many mistakes when it comes to you over the years and as badly as I wish that I could go back in time and ask you to be my wife then, I know that I can't."

"I've spent so many years chasing what has been right in front of me all along. I know that I still have ends to tie up on my end, but I promise that if you rock with me, you will always be a happy woman with me."

Pausing to study her face for a moment, he asked, "Will you please do me the honor of becoming my beautiful wife baby?"

In that moment, Rae released the ugliest cry of her life. Snot bubbles were present as she sobbed hysterically. She had been waiting for that man to ask her that question her entire life and here it was. He was divorcing his wife and actually wanted to be with her and their family. Once he managed to calm her down a bit, she then glanced around the room.

Her parents, his mom, little sister and her besties were tearful as well, while her brothers and Charlie nodded approvingly at her.

Finally redirecting her attention back at the man whose child, she was carrying in her womb, she screamed, "Yes Prosper! Hell yes, I will marry you baby!"

The room once again erupted into cheers as Prosper slid on the ring that he vowed to never make her want to take off.

∞

"Hurry up baby! I have literally three minutes to get there. I don't want to come off as unprofessional and keep them waiting for me." Rae urged her fiancée.

"Trust me, I'll get us there in one. We are about to turn on the street." He replied massaging her knee through her gown.

She glanced at him and smiled.

As he went to pull into his driveway, she couldn't help but to feel disappointed as she noticed that her potential buyer wasn't there yet. Trying to calm herself down, she reasoned that it wasn't quite time yet and to try to be patient. She'd give them thirty minutes before reaching out.

Prosper pulled into her garage so that he wasn't rubbing his relationship in to Claryssa or their nosy neighbors. He got out the car first and then went to let his bride to be out. He swiftly lifted her off her feet and carried her bridal style into the door that led to her house.

Rae was giggling as she basked in his attention. It felt so good to finally have her man all to herself.

Still holding Rae, Prosper started sucking on her neck and whispering to her that she should give him some before her appointment arrived. She told him no, but after she sealed the deal then he could have as much of her honey pot as he liked.

That was all he needed to hear. He would make sure that nothing got in the way of her sealing the deal in that case.

Stepping into her family room Rae released an alarmed scream which prompted Prosper to quickly investigate.

"Well, well, fucking well! If it isn't you two happy muthafucka!" A deranged Claryssa bellowed with a pistol pointed directly at Rae.

A scared PJ was sitting in a chair in the corner of the room.

"Aye Claryssa, what the fuck?! What are you doing?!" Prosper fumed.

"Oh, shut the fuck up! Did you actually think shit was just going to be hunky dory for the two of you...excuse me...the three of you?" She asked now pointing the gun at Rae's swollen midsection.

"Wait! C, you don't have to do this shit man. You don't have to do this. Please think about what you're doing especially in front of PJ. Look at her man...she is terrified. It's me that you are mad at. This is between us, don't put Desirae in the middle of our beef. Go home and I'll come with you. If you want, I can move back home. I didn't know that you were this upset by everything." Prosper attempted to reason with his estranged wife.

Claryssa blinked twice before releasing a laugh so eerie that the hair on the back of all of their necks stood at attention.

"You, you you! It is always about you! Fuck you!" She screamed loudly and her voice echoed through the large house.

PJ belted into a panicked scream. Both Prosper and Rae wanted to run up to and comfort the small child, however they knew better.

"I'm sorry to disappoint you this time hubby, but this shit here," she stated pointing between herself and Prosper, "Is so much bigger than you. This shit here is about Jazzy!"

"Who?!" Both Rae and Prosper exclaimed confused.

"Bitch, no one was even talking to your ass! And hubby, it's a shame that you are one of the people responsible for her death, yet you have the audacity to not even know who the fuck I'm talking about!" She screamed shooting him in his right leg.

"Argh!!!" Prosper yelled out, but then remembered his daughter was already frightened and held it in.

Attempting to control his pain through his breathing, he began to breathe in through his nose and out through his mouth.

He then said, "Claryssa please, I promise you, I do not know anyone named Jazzy. I swear!"

"Damn, that unfortunate, perhaps this will jog your memory." She stated she then aimed the gun at Rae's belly once again.

"This hoe won't be having this little bastard on my watch!" With that a loud succession of pops were heard followed deafening silence.

When Rae hit the ground, Prosper's heart fell into the pit of his stomach. He went to charge at Claryssa, but first noticed a look of horror in her eyes. As her drew closer, he noticed a trickle of blood at the corner of her mouth. She reached for him as her pistol hit the carpeted floor. He stepped backwards and watched as her pregnant body too hit the ground with a sickening thud. It wasn't until she faceplanted onto the ground that he noticed multiple hoes riddled into her back.

It was then that he realized that there was another shooter in the room. Panicking and attempting to protect himself and his daughter, he went to reach for the pistol that Claryssa had been carrying.

It was then that he heard a deep voice boom, "Nigga, don't even think about it. Back away from that gun!"

It dawned on him that it was Ant's voice talking to him. Listening to the other man's orders, Prosper backed away from the gun and waited for further instruction.

He then saw Ant walk into the room looking pissed. Ant put the gun away and immediately went to check on his sister.

He shook Rae and she instantly stood up and hugged her brother. PJ had run over to her father crying as he shielded her from her mother's dead body.

"Anybody want to tell me what the fuck is going on?" Prosper asked after no one bothered to say anything after a few moments.

"Yes Ant, what are you doing here?" Rae asked curiously as well.

"Well to make a long-complicated story short, I was dating Claryssa for about two years. We were very serious about each other too, or so I thought. I never understood why she was always so secretive with some aspects of her life. It all makes sense now, but at the time I believe her every word. She said that she was going through a divorce and that her husband was abusive. She didn't want to be seen with me in public because she didn't want anything negative getting back to his lawyers.

It wasn't until I seen her with you at Charlie's coming home party that I realized that she was a liar. I knew you and I knew that you weren't the type of husband that she made you out to be. At first, I started to be on some petty nigga shit, but I didn't want to hurt you...even if your married ass was creeping around with my little sister.

Instead, I decided to do my homework on her and to see what her angle was. I planted cameras here and Rae's house as well as at your house. Guess what I found out?!" Ant quizzed.

"What?! Both Rae and Prosper screamed in unison again.

"Remember the robbery that you and Charlie did years ago that put us all on and the chick that assisted y'all with the set up? Well her name was Jazmine and she was Claryssa's older sister. The two of them were extremely close and apparently Jazmine confided in Claryssa before she was killed. We all know that we didn't kill Jazmine, but unbeknownst to us, Clayssa blamed us all for her death."

"Holy shit!" Rae shouted in shock.

"Damn! Our entire marriage was a set up this entire time! She never fucking loved me. No wonder why she'd never let me meet her family. She was afraid of me seeing pictures and shit." Prosper exclaimed slowly putting the pieces together.

"Damn she was pregnant though..." Rae trailed sorrowfully while rubbing her own belly.

"Ha! Had this nigga been fucking his wife instead of smashing you, he would've realized that she was not pregnant." Ant said while turning Claryssa's body over, revealing a large prosthetic belly.

"Awww hell naw!!!" Prosper yelled out wondering who the fuck he had been married to.

"The bitch told me it was my baby too." Ant stood over her body and peered down at her hatefully.

"Baby, take PJ out of here." Rae said to Prosper as she began to stomp the hell out of the dead woman's body for hurting two of the most important men in her life.

"Yo what the fuck are you doing with your crazy ass girl?" Ant inquired.

"Mama, told us to never kick a bitch when she is down, so I'm stomping a hole into this hoe!" She fumed before her brother restrained her.

"Aye sis, you do know that since a murder has taken place in this house that I'm going to have to offer much less than I originally offered, right?" Ant said with a smirk.

With a huge smile on her face, she slapped her forehead because she should've realized that her brother was her mysterious buyer all along.

"Nuh unh negro, the shit was self-defense! Now run me my mon-ty!!!"

SHEENA PERRY

# The End

SHEENA PERRY

# Do No Harm: License To Kill

## *Is Coming soon!!!*

# Inevitable Deceptions: A Heart's Journey To Nowhere 3

*Is Coming soon!!!*

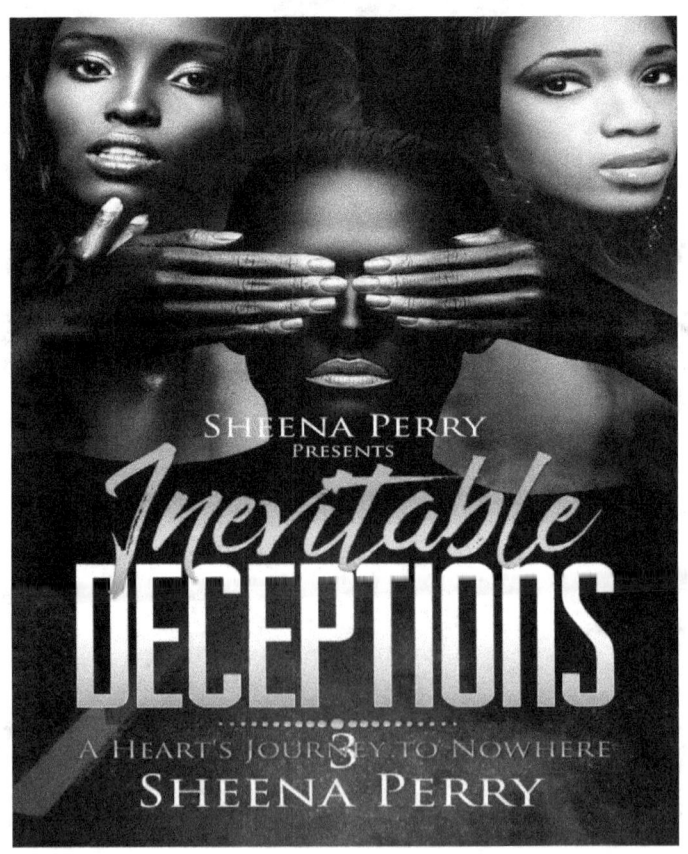

# Inevitable Deceptions: A Heart's Journey to Nowhere 1

## *Available Now!!!*

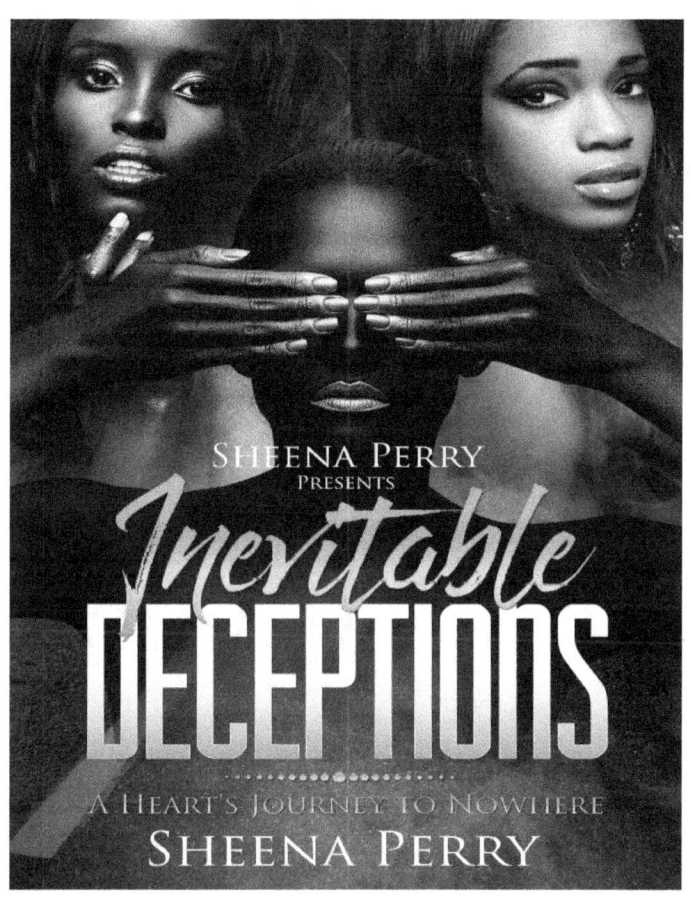

# Inevitable Deceptions: A Heart's Journey to Nowhere 2

## *Available Now!!!*

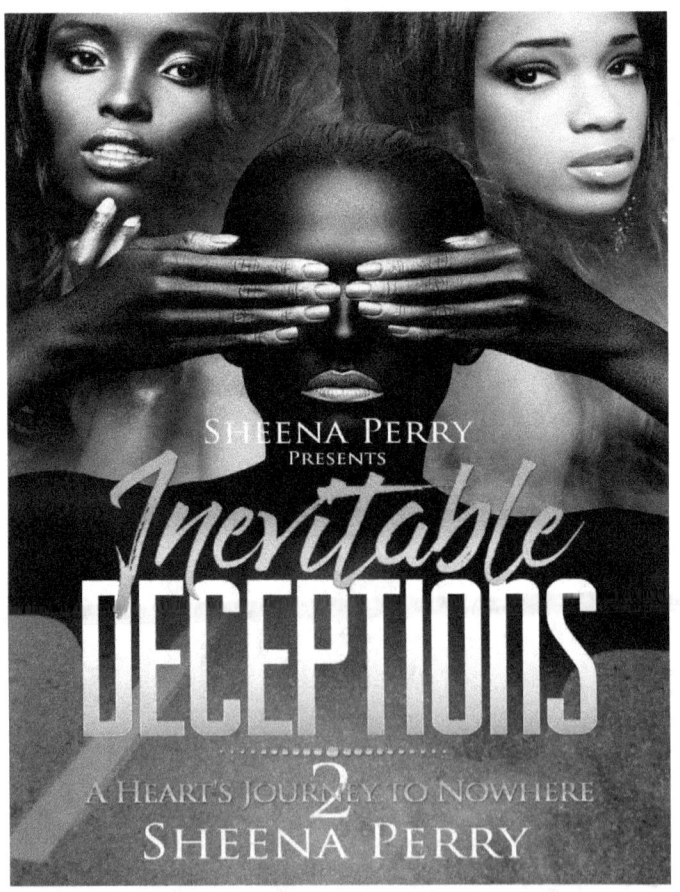

# My Wife's Daughters

## *Available Now!!!*

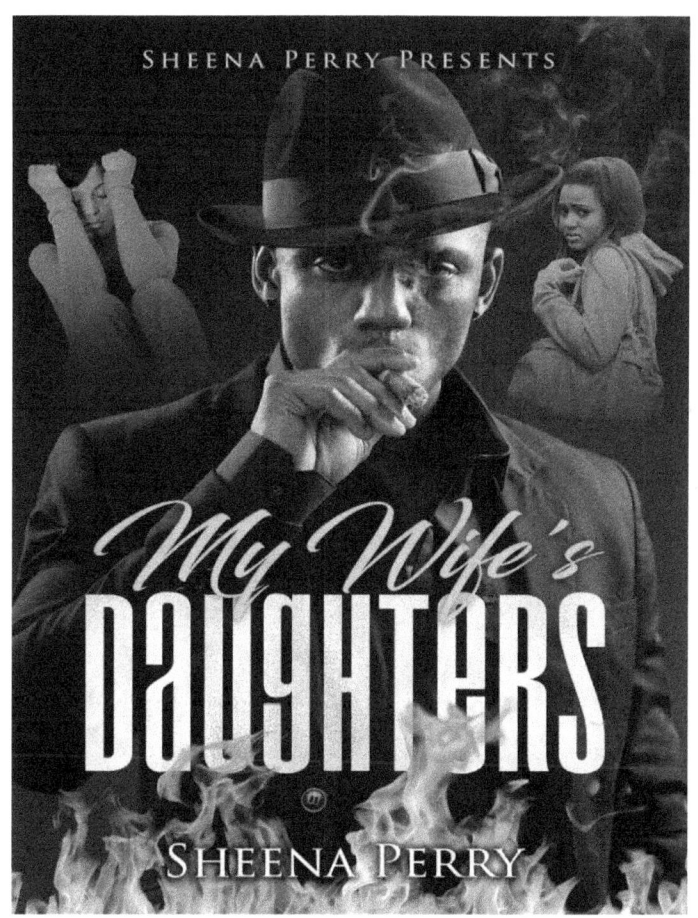

# They Call Me Junior: A Gay Love Story

## *Available Now!!!*

# They Call Me Junior: A Gay Love Story

*Available Now!!!*

# Releases From Other Authors

*Available Now!!!*

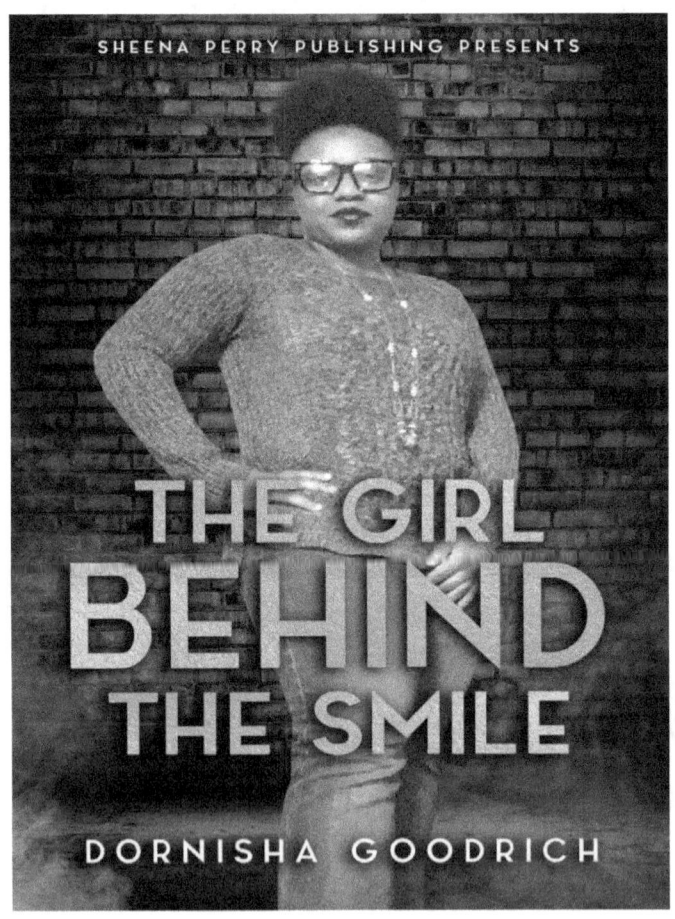

# Releases From Other Authors

## *Available Now!!!*

# Releases From Other Authors

## *Available Now!!!*

# Releases From Other Authors

*Is Coming soon!!!*

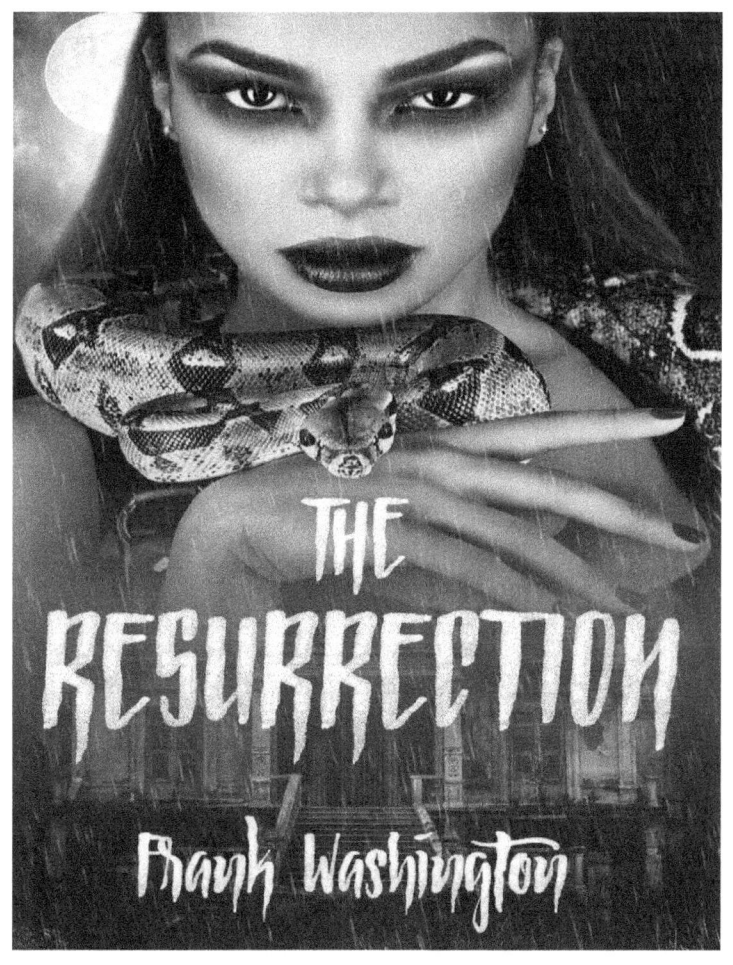

www.ingramcontent.com/pod-product-compliance
Lightning Source LLC
Chambersburg PA
CBHW071301250626
47159CB00004B/1259